GOODBYE, AUNT ELVA

ELIZABETH FENWICK

GOODBYE, AUNT ELVA

ATHENEUM *NEW YORK*

1968

GOODBYE, AUNT ELVA

CHAPTER ONE

"HERE SHE COMES," said Roddy, from the window.

His mother stirred without rising. His tone was not urgent.

He went on, still leisurely, "Just turned the corner. Trot, trot. What a little bag of bones she is."

She said nothing.

"I see what you mean about the paint job. God, it looks like neon, doesn't it? Old ladies shouldn't use red, there's nothing in their skin to match it. Pink, maybe. Or lavender."

He laughed. Behind him, she got up, and he turned to look at her.

"You're sure that's a wig?"

"Yes."

"Well. All right, over to you. I'll be in the kitchen."

"No, go upstairs," she said. "And be quiet, Roddy."

She stopped by a dim mirror, smoothing her own hair, which was full enough for a wig, dark enough for a dye job, and yet was neither. Nor had her sallow skin begun to leach out; she could still wear color if she wanted to, she could even dominate her customary black. Grateful for this hereditary promise, he gave her solid waist a squeeze as he went by. Her too-solid waist. Like his. Well, you couldn't keep everything.

3

She paid no real attention to him, and not much to herself. The tidying was perfunctory. What she did was to look into her own dark eyes for a moment—a still moment—and then go to open the front door. She went just outside, leaving the door slightly ajar, and waited on the porch.

The old porch, sagging under bloomless wistaria vines, limited her view as it limited the inward view of passers-by and deadened somewhat the traffic echoes from the next street over. This was the business street, the downtown section, of their small New England city: solid with stores and buildings, some of them three and four stories high. Decay lay here behind it, and some confusion. A couple of apartment houses had gone up some years ago, and were still filled with people who wanted to be close to work, or older people who liked being near "everything." There was a large parking lot across the street, giving access to the backs of stores. Yet some of the old homes survived, especially on this, the far side of the street. But these were mostly in poor repair, and few kept their original tenants. Families with too many children, anonymous solitary roomers, came and went. Now the houses themselves were beginning to go, and newer apartments to go up.

There was one next door, aggressive with raw brick and cement balconies. The brisk, unsteady heeltaps were going toward it, passing the wistaria-drowned porch.

The woman standing there stepped forward and spoke. "Good morning," she said levelly. "Miss Besserman."

"Oh!"

4

The small woman stopped abruptly—teetered, clutching her shopping bag, then desperately smiled.

"Oh—good morning . . . Good morning, Mrs. Kay! I'm afraid I didn't see you at first, your lovely vines . . ."

She looked at them doubtfully, then stretched another smile.

"Such nice weather, isn't it?"

"I was hoping you'd come by, Miss Besserman."

"Oh? Oh, well, you can pretty well count on me, you know—morning shopping, rain or shine, a little breath of fresh air . . ."

Her painted eyes, above all this, said simply: What?

"I wonder if you'd have time to come in a moment?"

The eyes closed down, turned away. In confusion, rather than refusal. Miss Besserman's bare little life feared the impromptu; only the known was safe. Besides, as the woman watching her knew, she was slightly ashamed of her one visit to this house, because she had come to have her fortune told in cards. Only for fun, of course. She did not really believe in magic. Now she looked as if she were afraid of being blackmailed.

"Something's come up," said Mrs. Kay. "I'd value your advice."

"Oh? Oh, dear—no trouble, I hope?"

Is it money? said the eyes.

"No, no," said Mrs. Kay. "There might be a little profit in it for you."

This was a mistake. Miss Besserman made an almost convulsive retreat.

"Oh—oh, thank you, but you know I'm quite retired

5

—I'm awfully stubborn about that, I'm afraid. Besides . . ."

Besides, why do you need a retired saleslady?

Mrs. Kay gave her a broad smile, coaxing.

"Oh, this is something new for you," she promised. "You might be surprised. Anyway, come in and have a cup of coffee."

She opened her screen door then and stood holding it, smiling. Miss Besserman, trapped by courtesy, teetered a few steps in obedience and then stopped.

"I'll just take these things home, first. . . . They should go in the refrigerator. . . ."

She would never come back. An incoherent telephone call would end the matter.

"Put them in mine," said Mrs. Kay, still firmly smiling. "No bother."

She continued to hold the door. Defeated, Miss Besserman showed courage. She smiled back, an impossibly red-and-white smile, and said almost gaily:

"Well, how nice of you. Just for a minute, then."

"Watch the steps," Mrs. Kay replied, her eyes falling to Miss Besserman's little bird-feet in their high-heeled shoes.

It was good advice. The unpainted boards sagged, showed wide cracks to catch narrow heels. Miss Besserman eyed them anxiously, and took care. The porch's camber made her stagger just at first.

She said doggedly, "These dear old homes—what histories they must have"; and then flinched under Mrs. Kay's guiding hand that closed around her arm.

"Just go on through. The sun's in the back now, and I

6

know you like to look out on the garden."

"Oh, indeed I do."

The sun was certainly not in the front of the house. A gloomy hallway, flanked by one closed sliding door and one glimpse of somber furnishings, invited no pause. Mrs. Kay made none, but resolutely led her guest through the open room and a massive dark dining room behind it. Beyond this, filtering pale light invaded a smaller room whose many windows looked out, mostly, on the pressing greenery of an old and neglected garden. A round table with an oilcloth cover had three assorted chairs drawn around it, two of rattan and one old Morris chair, each provided with faded cushions. Clearly this was, or has been, a favored retreat.

Miss Besserman said, "How pleasant . . . Wasn't this where we . . . ?"

"Yes, this is my nook. Nicer with the sun on it, isn't it? Sit down, Miss Besserman. I'll put your groceries in the icebox for you, and get us some coffee."

Left alone, Miss Besserman leaned and looked upward, searching for the reassuring sight of her own windows, three stories up in the apartment house that loomed next door. But the shrubbery was too thick, the angle wrong; she would have needed to rise and peer, and of course she did no such thing. Instead her blinking glance went around the small room and stopped at the Morris chair, with its enormous standard ashtray beside it. A man's chair; a man's ashtray. Used, emptied, but not washed for a long time. Miss Besserman had not been able to decide if the heavy dark man she occasionally glimpsed was hired help or a roomer. He cut the

7

lawn, infrequently, indifferently, with a rusty hand mower. Once she had seen him clumsily pounding nails into the back steps. The yard seemed to have no other care.

Yet still, in spring, the lilacs bloomed at impossible plumy heights. Purple and white, the lovely old-fashioned kind. That had been her first view out of the little paint-smelling boxy room that was to be her new home, and Miss Besserman's heart had lifted at such luck. How much richer she would be, after all, than the tenants in front with their balconies and street view she could not afford. What was their view compared to hers? Traffic, backs of stores, parking lot and each other. She had lilacs —grass, shrubbery, and who knew what else to come?

Actually, nothing else had come. An old peony bed that she had spotted came up, but failed to bloom. Nascent day-lilies became lost in a fall of untied climbing-rose canes; and these, overshadowed in turn, scarcely bloomed. Yet, tangled and uncared for though it was, the old garden remained her cherished view. Birds came there (and cats), and crickets were beginning to call, with the cooling nights, and the wind-whispering leaves of the charming old cut-leaf maple were just beginning to turn. The fact that no one else seemed to care for the garden gave it a deepened personal value to her, in time. But she did not think much of the yard man, whoever he was. Her glance came back to the huge, soiled ashtray and flicked away again.

Mrs. Kay reappeared from what seemed to be an adjoining pantry, and brought a tray to the table—serving out its contents before sitting down, as if they were in a cafeteria. She discouraged Miss Besserman's offer to help. The coffeepot was a perfectly lovely piece of old china, and Miss Besserman exclaimed over it.

"Yes," said Mrs. Kay, matter-of-fact. "The doctor had lots of nice things. I don't know what will become of them if the house goes. Nobody wants old things any more."

"Oh, but I think this must be a very fine piece," said Miss Besserman. "Surely . . ." She paused. "If the house goes? Aren't you going to keep it?"

"They want to build another apartment here," said Mrs. Kay.

"Oh, *no!*"

"Yes. Right up against yours. They don't care any more if people have to stare out one window right into another. I suppose they'll leave you enough airspace to breathe—there must be some kind of law about it. But you'll miss your view, won't you? I often see you sitting up there, looking out and enjoying it."

Miss Besserman received her deliberate words numbly, aware of some intent behind them, yet too crushed to care what it was. She did not doubt that they wanted to build another apartment house here; the wonder was that her garden had survived for so long. Already she could see the bricks coming up, walling her in alive, like someone in an Edgar Allan Poe story. And she could not afford to move again. Besides, where would she go?

She looked sadly into Mrs. Kay's waiting eyes.

"Is this what you wanted to tell me?"

"Yes, it is. I knew you wouldn't want a thing like that to happen if you could help it. You don't, do you?"

9

Miss Besserman was not yet capable of speech. Allowing her time, Mrs. Kay attended to her own coffee and then pushed the plastic pitcher and bowl along the oilcloth.

"Pull yourself together, we're not licked yet," she said kindly. "Take a little cream, Miss Besserman."

CHAPTER TWO

THE CREAM WAS canned milk. Perceiving this just
in time, Miss Besserman put the pitcher down again
and, in a convulsive movement, drank quite a lot of the
black coffee from her cup. It was very bitter, and calmed
her at once. Like accepting an unpalatable truth.

"I will certainly sign any petition you have in mind,
Mrs. Kay," she said then. "I'm not a petition-signer generally, but I think this is an exception. It's perfectly out-
rageous they should want to take your house away from
you like this! How can they do it?"

Mrs. Kay, though attentive, did not reply to this at
once. She said at length, almost absently: "Why, no one
wants you to sign anything, Miss Besserman. You
wouldn't be asked to sign anything."

"I'm perfectly willing," Miss Besserman replied
firmly. "I assure you, I am."

She felt the bravery of commitment flowing into her,
sitting there opposite this slow and thoughtful woman in
her threatened home. Mrs. Kay only nodded, in some
sort of general acknowledgment.

Then she said: "This could all blow over in no time,
you know. If they can't get this land, then they'll build a
smaller apartment house on the two lots the other side of
us. You'd still have your open space, and the garden to

look out on—nobody'd bother about it then. Sixty feet, what could they make out of it but a parking lot? Nobody's going to bother about that. As soon as they give up and build the smaller building, that's the end of it. You understand? And they're not going to wait much longer for this place."

"I understand," said Miss Besserman, keenly attentive. "A delaying action. Isn't that what you mean?"

"It's exactly what I mean. You're a smart woman. I knew you were."

"How can I help?" Miss Besserman asked simply.

Mrs. Kay poured more coffee into their cups from the pretty pot. Miss Besserman at once drank hers. She had begun almost to relish the uncompromising black brew . . . and the sense of alliance with this woman defending her home against the bulldozers or whatever they were. Women need not always be helpless before the destroyers of gardens!

"There's a fellow, a lawyer or something, coming here to try and talk Mrs. Ryan out of her rights," Mrs. Kay said, very slowly. "She's an old lady, and not able to stand up to it. You could talk for her, Miss Besserman. Send him away with a flea in his ear, like she would if she could. That's all you have to do. That'll be the end of it. Just keep saying No—and No. If she objects, he can't do a thing."

Miss Besserman comprehended so little of this, and was so repelled by the little she did understand, that she sat impassive. At the same time she felt her brief excitement ooze right out of her, and all bravery with it.

To conceal this, she said the first thing that came into her head.

"Who is Mrs. Ryan?" she asked—and felt a horrid, silly smile twitch at her lips.

Mrs. Kay put her head on one side.

"Why, that's right," she said "I keep forgetting how new you are around here. You don't remember when Dr. Ryan lived here. That was his office, the other side of the house. Elva was his second wife—there was a divorce, and children, and about all he could leave her was the right to live in this house as long as she lived. If she could scrape up the money to do it. She couldn't even have done that if I hadn't come and lived here and shared expenses with her. And helped her keep the place up. *And* looked after her too, these past years she's been so feeble. Now it would pretty well finish her if they snatched her out of this place and stuck her somewhere among strangers—and you can bet that's what they'd do, those Ryans."

"Dear, dear," Miss Besserman murmured, feeling that mindless smile still flickering at her lips. Under Mrs. Kay's grave gaze she made a heroic effort to control it.

Mrs. Kay seemed to approve the result. She leaned closer, over the table.

"I have my home to lose too, and my place of business," she said frankly. "Just like you've got your view—and I know that means a lot to you. I remember how you talked about it, the night you were here.

(Oh, what—*what* had she said?)

"But don't forget, that old lady has the most to lose of all," Mrs. Kay continued. "She wouldn't live through a cruel thing like that. It would be the death of her, that's all. She wouldn't survive it."

Miss Besserman, still sitting erect on her side of the

13

table, felt that already brick walls were rising around her, enclosing her completely. They were made of Mrs. Kay's unanswerable, incomprehensible words. If she did not break through at once with words of her own, she would never escape.

She said, very fast, "Mrs. Kay, I am in no position to speak to a strange lawyer on behalf of a strange woman. He would pay no attention to me. Why should he?"

"He would pay attention to you if he thought you were Elva," Mrs. Kay replied unbelievably. "And that's exactly what he would think. Why wouldn't he?"

"If he thought I were Mrs. Ryan?"

"Certainly—what else would he think? You'd simply be here, sitting in her chair—there isn't a one of them has laid eyes on her in years. And I could fix you up to fool anybody who had, don't worry about that. You've only to sit there and say to him what Elva would say to him herself if she could—that you don't agree, and you're not going out of the house. There's not a thing in this world he can do then but get out. Why, I should think you'd *enjoy* squashing a wicked scheme like that, with no more than a few minutes, and a couple of words! Even if it meant nothing to you at all, Miss Besserman. Just for the charity of it. Even if it had nothing at all to do with saving your garden."

Miss Besserman sat and heard her out, almost tranquil with shock. She heard her own voice float out into the air between them.

"I couldn't do it, Mrs. Kay. I'm very sorry."

With no change of expression Mrs. Kay got out of her chair.

14

"I want you to come with me, just for a minute," she said. "I want to show you something."

Miss Besserman sat on, looking up at her.

"I'm sorry. I couldn't do it."

"Just for a moment. Surely you can spare one more minute before you go. Come along, get up, Miss Besserman," she added more sharply.

Suddenly flushing, Miss Besserman got to her feet. Only, the rattan chair was tippy, difficult to leave, and Mrs. Kay's arm supported her to steadiness.

She stood very still, but Mrs. Kay's arm remained.

"May I please have my groceries now, Mrs. Kay."

"Of course. Come along."

"I'm quite all right."

She meant, Don't hold me. Mrs. Kay at once dropped her arm.

"Yes. This way."

And she went deliberately away through the dim dining and sitting rooms, and disappeared.

Miss Besserman, taken by surprise, remained obstinately immobile. Then, in an unsteady scurry, she followed. As she reached the hall, Mrs. Kay was climbing the stairs.

"Mrs. Kay—my things—"

Her voice came out such a wail that Mrs. Kay turned and looked down at her. Miss Besserman put a shamed hand to her cheek, almost whispering.

"You have my groceries in your refrigerator. . . ."

"Don't worry, I haven't forgotten. But you won't want to carry them around the house, Miss Besserman."

She stood looking down, so reasonable and surprised,

that a kind of dizziness took hold of Miss Besserman. She could not think what was the matter, what was right.

Then she thought, yielding, Well, it's only a . . . I'll just . . . and then simply go, that's all.

She put her hand on the railing, and began a reluctant ascent. Mrs. Kay nodded, and went on ahead of her.

When Miss Besserman reached the top Mrs. Kay was at one end of the narrow hall, waiting with her hand upon a doorknob. She held a finger up, then slowly motioned with it. What did she mean?

With weary dignity, Miss Besserman came on; and as she approached the door Mrs. Kay pushed it open.

A sunny room, at the back of the house. Very crowded with things. A white-painted iron bedstead, with its foot towards the door. An old wheelchair, empty, nearby.

"Go on in," Mrs. Kay encouraged, beside her. "It doesn't matter if she's awake or sleeping, it's all the same to her. She likes to see people. Go on, dear."

To end it, Miss Besserman stepped just inside. An old, old woman lay in the bed, sunken eyes closed, sunken mouth fallen slack. Thin, thin hands upon her covered chest. She showed no sign of life at all.

Mrs. Kay had brought her up here to see a dead woman. *Didn't she know it?*

Mute with horror, unable to move, Miss Besserman watched Mrs. Kay go up to that inert body and begin to handle and urge it, as if to make it live again. She patted and rubbed the hands, patted the cheeks, took hold of the bony face and moved it from side to side. . . .

"Oh, *don't*," Miss Besserman whispered.

The eyes came open and stared upward, pale and

wild. The mouth began to work, faint hoarse sounds is-
sued from it and mingled with the real voice of the living woman leaning over the bed—still briskly talking, as
her hands still urged and patted.

"That's right, that's a good girl. You've got someone
come to see you, a visitor, isn't that nice? Aren't you
going to say hello? Haven't you got a nice smile to say
hello?"

The pale eyes wavered around and discovered Miss
Besserman where she stood shrinking in upon herself.
They saw her. For a long moment that pale, unearthly
gaze remained fixed upon Miss Besserman's face. Then,
hoarsely croaking again, the fallen mouth stretched itself
into a wide and toothless smile.

It was smiling at her.

With a choking cry, Miss Besserman wheeled around
and shot out the door. Her own vision had come unfo-
cused, her legs staggered beneath her—she struck against
the doorframe and rebounded, reeling, into the narrow
hall. Struck against something else and cried out again—
and was caught.

Caught, held. Imprisoned. Two enormous, hot hands
seized her by the arms, a great male body blocked hers, a
man's dark face stared hugely down at her. Other hands
laid hold of her from behind, and a jostle of large bodies
seemed to engulf her failing body. Laconic voices over-
laced her feeble cries.

She felt her coiffure slipping, endangering her sight,
and she tried to raise her hands and could not. Cool air
swept over her entire head, as she was lifted from the
floor and carried away.

CHAPTER THREE

Miss besserman lay on a velvet settee, weeping.

She wept in hopeless sorrow, no longer in hysteria; she made no noise, and Mrs. Kay no longer restrained her in any way. The man was gone. It made no difference. Years of unshed, unsuspected tears flowed from Miss Besserman's swollen eyes, and she made no attempt to conceal them.

Nor did she care any longer that Mrs. Kay sat so close beside her and continued to scold. Miss Besserman, with her hand to her mouth and her head turned away, let the scolding words flow past her. Her eyes remained closed; only the flow of tears betrayed her returned consciousness; but Mrs. Kay was well aware of it.

"You might have frightened the poor old thing to death," she was saying now. "I'm ashamed for you, Miss Besserman—I took you for a woman of refinement, and kindness. Screeching out that way, and running out of the room! From an old lady that's only trying to make you welcome. It isn't her fault she doesn't speak well, she does her best, she has her feelings. I'm ashamed of you!"

A shuddering moan escaped Miss Besserman. Mrs. Kay paused; but when no words came she went on, remorseless:

"She's a human woman, same as either one of us, only a bit further along is all. We might any one of us come

to it someday—and how would you like to have someone . . ."

You thought I look like that, Miss Besserman cried
out, without sound. Mrs. Kay swept on.

". . . screeching and running away from you like you
were a wicked witch instead of a good, helpless old lady
that never harmed a soul?"

"You thought— You think—"

Mrs. Kay leaned down; but no more words came.
After a moment, from beneath a shielding hand, Miss
Besserman whispered:

"My dentures . . ."

Mrs. Kay moved back.

"I told you, Roddy's looking for them. They must
have gone down the stairs. You'd have gone down yourself, most likely, if he hadn't caught hold of you. I don't
know what you can expect if you fling yourself around
and carry on like that! All I hope is that they're still in
one piece—and you'd better be grateful you are yourself."

But they could not have come out so easily. Only this
morning she had put them in carefully, with the Shur-
Tite . . . hadn't she? Besides, her mouth was sore. It
was sore.

Miss Besserman wept.

She wept into silence. Mrs. Kay seemed to have tired
of talking to her—tired even of sitting there, for there
were sounds of her getting up. Presently she began to
walk away.

In sudden panic, Miss Besserman half rose, calling
after her.

"Mrs. Kay—?"

She put her hand over her mouth again, quickly, as the other turned; but Mrs. Kay still looked at her with a kind of surprise—disapproving surprise. Then she shook her head.

"Honestly, look what you've done to yourself," she said, less crossly. "A pretty little woman like you, all smeared up like that. Come on, let's tidy you up."

Miss Besserman, unreasonably, shrank from her return. But when the broad hand came down, she helplessly took it—preventing, perhaps, its taking hold of her. There was a dizzying moment of rise, and then she was unsteadily on her feet. Her stockinged feet.

"My shoes . . ."

"Right there, dear," said Mrs. Kay. And there were, her shoes, fallen on their sides by the velvet settee. "Don't put them on yet, though—you're not steady enough for those heels. Anyway, it's all carpet—just over here."

Diminished, Miss Besserman crept across a big, old-fashioned bedroom and let herself be put onto a bench. Her wandering gaze was taking in the massive furniture, the heavy draperies, the loss of all lovely sunlight—or did that mean they were at the other end of the house now? *From that room.* Oh, she hoped so!

Suddenly the woman in the mirror leaped out at her.

She gave one cry, and covered her face with both hands.

Mrs. Kay dropped something, and breathed rather heavily while she recovered it. Her hands, then, taking down Miss Besserman's hands, were very brisk.

But her tone was still mild as she remarked, "My, you

20

are a nervous one, aren't you—who in the world did you think it was? It's only us."

Miss Besserman knew better than to risk another look at the reflected Mrs. Kay—and the wild white hair, the smeared and shrunken face below it.

"Oh—oh," she gasped, screwing her eyes up tight.

Mrs. Kay was opening drawers, rummaging in them.

"Well, I told you you needed tidying. Now sit still and let me do it."

"Let me go home—I want to go home—"

"Not looking like this, you don't. Good lord, how you've smeared yourself up! You look like a little Indian. I hope I can get it off. . . . But you mustn't squint like that," she said, impersonal. "Smooth out—that's right, keep your eyes shut, but smooth out. That's better."

"There," she said, deftly wiping cream, or oil, from Miss Besserman's frozen countenance. "There, it's coming. One more cleaning and we'll have you as good as new. Then you'll see how nice I can make you look, just as you are. You'll see."

They had taken her coiffure, too. Everything. How had it all happened so quickly? Where had everything gone?

A brush went through her hair, snapping her head back. At once a firm hand supported her neck, and the brush came back more carefully.

Above her, Mrs. Kay grunted: "Sorry, I didn't realize it was so th—so fine. Didn't hurt you, did I, dear?"

What else had they taken? Her shoes . . . no; but her groceries? Her bag? Her bag!

Miss Besserman's eyes flew open.

"Where is my bag?"

"Your bag?"

The brush paused. Then, with a clatter, it fell on the dressing table—thrown down, before Mrs. Kay stalked away. Miss Besserman warily watched her go.

She did not leave the room—only jerked the door open and called in a commanding voice:

"Roddy!"

She waited, and called again. Miss Besserman, listening intently, heard nothing; but apparently Mrs. Kay did, for she went on as if she had been answered:

"Bring that stuff up here, so Miss Besserman can see it. Now, please."

She shut the door and came back heavy and expressionless. Picked up the brush and went rather painfully to work again.

Miss Besserman would not let herself be intimidated.

She said doggedly, "I would like my coiffure, too, please."

"You'll have what's yours, Miss Besserman. We're not thieves here."

In hostile silence the tidying continued, and Miss Besserman continued miserably not to watch. Before long heavy footsteps became audible, and then the door was flung open. Miss Besserman's eyes flew open too.

In the mirror she saw the dark man, looming in the doorway. He was carrying her handbag, nothing else, and he stood there and looked back at her in the mirror.

"Bring it here, please, Roddy," said Mrs. Kay. "Give it to Miss Besserman. Did you find her teeth?"

"Sure," he said, coming slowly across the room. "Hey, that looks pretty good."

Miss Besserman's bag dropped into her lap. She clutched it to her.

"I'm not finished yet. Where's her teeth?" she asked again.

"Well, she knocked one of them out. I re-set it for her, but it's got to dry. Should have twenty-four hours, really."

"*Oh!*"

Miss Besserman exhaled her long-held breath. Neither of them paid any attention to her.

"And the wig—where's the wig?" Mrs. Kay went on, prompting.

"Well, that's a little more of a problem. It fell into Aunt Elva's slopjar. I don't know what to do about it. Do you wash them, or what?"

"Oн!"

This time it was a cry of anguish, and disbelief. And of sudden helplessness. Mother and son stood looking down at her.

Mrs. Kay said, "She's very nervous, Roddy. Better leave us awhile."

He made a gesture of compliance and wandered away, after another curious glance in the mirror. When he was gone Miss Besserman looked up, her eyes filling with tears.

"Oh—*what is it?*" she said. "What do you want?"

Mrs. Kay's hand passed over her hair, a proprietary gesture. She said in a coaxing voice,

"Now take a look at yourself, Miss Besserman. Violet.

Come on, just take a look."

Miss Besserman looked. She saw a still old woman, sitting under the presence of that large, and equally still, other woman. A tidy old woman; clean, entirely rational, and sad. Who would not have frightened anyone who came upon her.

"I want to add a little delicate color," Mrs. Kay said, considering. "And your eyes will look much better when they're rested. I'll put some pads on them, to help bring down the swelling. You have a very sweet face, Violet—you should be glad."

Miss Besserman's lips trembled.

"I thought you wanted to make me look . . . like her. . . ."

"What an idea! Why would I do that?" Mrs. Kay became busy again, looking in the backs of the drawers. She went on: "It isn't really her looks that's the trouble, though, it's her poor mind. Anyway, you couldn't look like her—you're a much younger woman, and very well preserved too. You know that. No, it's more a matter of size, and the bone structure, you might say. There aren't so many really *dainty* women—of a possible age, and with a good, kind disposition. And ladylike. The rest of it's nothing—only a matter of making up, like for a play. You'll just be playing Elva Ryan the way she ought to be," Mrs. Kay said, smiling now. "There's plenty of women in their eighties that are full of life and go—it's just that poor Elva's not one of them. *You'll* be one of them—I'll make you that bet right now, for any sum you want to name. And pay off gladly, if *I'm* still around in twenty years!"

She did not expect this gross flattery to be believed, Miss Besserman thought sadly. Did not even care if it was. She was only good-natured with relief because she thought Miss Besserman had given in. So easily intimidated, and so soon. Without making them do—whatever else they might do.

In true wonder, she looked at the reflected woman standing over her.

"When will he come, Mrs. Kay?" she asked. "This—person?"

"You mean the lawyer? When I tell him he can," Mrs. Kay said grandly. "Whenever you like. Take a little time to rest first," she added, cautious once more. "So you won't be nervous. A good night's sleep ought to do it."

"Here?"

"Well, you don't want to go out till you get fixed up again, do you? Till Roddy gets your things fixed. You'll be perfectly comfortable here."

"Do you promise I can go home again, afterwards?"

Mrs. Kay seemed surprised, not pleased, by this question.

"Promise! What is there to promise about?" she said coldly. "You have your home and we have ours—and we both want to keep them as they are. Garden and all. Isn't that it?"

"I—I suppose so."

If only they were not so *big*. In exhaustion, in confusion, Miss Besserman forced her eyes away from that looming reflection.

"I'd like to rest awhile," she said humbly.

Mrs. Kay received the idea with approval.

"I think you should. Just stretch out, and I'll bring you a coverlet. And when you wake up, I'll bring you a nice tray. Do you want the bathroom?"

Even this humiliation was not spared her. Miss Besserman did. She was guided down the hall, left shut in alone. But when she came out and stood hesitant, Roddy put his head around a nearby door.

"Okay, Miss Besserman?"

She nodded. He was wasting his time. She wanted nothing more than to creep back into whatever privacy she could command, and shut behind her the door that had no key.

CHAPTER FOUR

I AM NOT Elva Ryan. I am Violet Besserman, and I live next door. Please take me home at once—ring the superintendent's bell, he knows me, he will tell you who I am!"

But would he know her . . . like this?

In sudden doubt, Miss Besserman canceled her silent speech. The shadowy lawyer to whom she was speaking faded away, into the shadows of the strange bedroom. Not yet; not yet.

She needed more time to think. *And her teeth.*

They must let me have my dentures before he comes, Miss Besserman thought. That is only reasonable. I can't talk to anyone without them—I won't try!

At least her mind was clear now. It was not tranquil— how could it be?—nor was it working perfectly, but raced and stalled and raced again into blind alleys. Still, she must take what chance she could to think her way out of this dreadful situation before it got any worse.

She must have slept all day—if it was sleeping. The room lay shadowed around her, except for the light of the street lamp coming in through long, heavy draperies. Her watch was still on her wrist, she was relieved to see, but she could not read it. Nor did she want to turn on a light, lest they notice she was awake and come in and frighten her witless once more, before she had thought things out.

Very cautiously, she slid from the bed, crept over to the window. How many lights there were, across the parking lot! And how many cars still there. So the stores were still open. And there was someone walking along below her, passing the porch, going on into the tree shadows beyond. She could hear his footsteps through the closed window.

Why should she not open it? Call out for help?

Miss Besserman leaned forward, her hands at the windowframe, and stared down intently. Waiting for the next one.

Then she shrank back. As if from momentary but dangerous vertigo. Impossible, impossible. Shrieking out the window, like some demented old person—she could not do it.

Even if she did, probably no one would come but Mrs. Kay. Or the man Roddy. When she thought of them, the last of Miss Besserman's courage expired. She feared them now—she physically feared them; and there was not any use pretending that she did not.

Her feet were getting chilly. She tiptoed back to the bed—how everything creaked, in this house!—and sat on the edge of it, wrapping her legs in the quilt. She felt surprisingly well (although hungry) after her long period of unconsciousness, and the determination returned to her *not* to pretend to be an old woman called Elva Ryan.

If only she *looked* more like herself!

Miss Besserman sat on the bed awhile longer. She

28

would very much have liked some light in the room, to go back to the dressing table and its mirror. She still had her handbag, and there were a few little things in there.

Presently she went back and pulled down the windowblinds. One of them simply unrolled and hung limp; clearly the spring was gone, she would never get it back up. Well, that was another day's problem. She groped her way carefully across the pitch-black room and, at last, found the dressing-table lamp and switched it on.

Without a glance at her reflection, Miss Besserman sat down and began selecting what she needed from her bag. A flat compact of Heavenly Blush—that would need a little water. The tube of Foxtone, for the lashes, since her coiffure was a reddish gold. Her eyebrow pencil, in Mod Brown, and a tube of Foxfire, for the lips, and Overshine, to cover the Foxfire. Hardly any of these had had much use, but Miss Besserman had thought it wise always to carry them in case she might be away from home awhile. Indeed, she thought wryly, one never knew.

She laid out these allies before her, and then took up the brush which Mrs. Kay had used. At the edge of her attention, unexamined, moved the ghostly shape of her whole reflection. She had no use for it. Only the young like to sit and stare at themselves; she had long ago learned to work from one small, carefully tended area to the next. Even her final inspection in a long mirror (for which she put on her glasses) was mainly for hems and stocking seams. After all, the parts made up the whole.

When she had given her hair a kind of spirited tidying, she looked around for water. There was not a drop, not so much as a drinking glass.

Well, she was entitled to use the bathroom. If she turned on only the tiniest stream of water, to dampen her sponge, there was no reason they should hear her.

Still she hesitated a long while before opening the door into the hall. When she finally peered out, it was into deep gloom streaked only by some reflected light coming up the stairs. No sound at all.

Miss Besserman darted out, shoeless and silent.

She made the bathroom unchallenged. Cautiously latched the door, and then spent some time groping on the wall for a light-switch. It seemed there was none. But old recollection came to her aid and she found her way to the sink and the dangling chain above it. She managed all this without the slightest betraying sound.

The shock was doubled, then, when her first cautious turn of the tap produced a groan that seemed to shake the walls. Instantly she turned the tap off again. The groan shuddered away. Miss Besserman stood very still, then hurried into action.

She had just, with shaking haste, begun dampening her sponge pad in the puddle of water left in the sink when she heard someone coming up the stairs. Along the hall.

"Miss Besserman!"

Mrs. Kay's voice offered tentative friendliness.

"You all right in there?"

"Yes . . . ! All right . . . thank you."

"Want a little supper? I'll bring you up a tray, you

needn't come down."

"No. Yes, please!" She recollected herself. "But I must have my dentures, Mrs. Kay. I can't manage without them."

"Don't you worry, you'll be fine. I'll get you some night things too, nice and warm."

Mrs. Kay tramped away, without touching the door. Went back downstairs.

Instantly, Miss Besserman emerged and sped back to her room, swept all her beauty aids into her handbag, and took everything back to the bathroom without, it seemed, drawing one full breath. At least they would not take these away from her. Dizzy, she sat on the edge of the tub and waited. Time went by.

Presently, a little courage returned to her. Since she was known to be here, she might as well use the facilities. She rose and did so, pulling the noisy lavatory chain with shrinking distaste, turning on the groaning water once more. (But, turned on full, it made no noise. Now she knew.) She even extracted her Heavenly Blush once more and began a determined use of it, not to waste that chance of water.

They came back while she was dabbing—both of them, a floor-shaking invasion, their heavy voices antiphonal and unclear beyond the door. Silver and dishes rattled, drawers slammed, more footsteps . . . and awful pauses.

Then Mrs. Kay's voice outside the bathroom again (while the other one clumped downstairs, thank goodness).

"You're sure you're all right, now, Miss Besserman?"

"Yes—all right—"

"Give a call if you want anything, we're right downstairs, we'll hear you. And don't let your supper get cold."

"Good night, then. See you in the morning."

"Good night . . ."

Oh, how awful to be such a coward! To feel so small, and weak, only at the sound of them . . . And she had made such a poor job of her Heavenly Blush, too, putting it on with her hands shaking, and too much water, and—all streaky, like *clown* makeup. . . .

Incautiously staring, Miss Besserman now saw that more was wrong than the Heavenly Blush. Was that really all that was left of her hair—those unmanageable white wisps, uncurled, lifeless? Turning away, shaken, Miss Besserman thought: I must leave it uncovered more, it's lost its body—there must be some sort of strengthener to use . . . and put it up, perhaps a home permanent . . .?

But she felt unaccountably discouraged, trailing back down the hall to her room.

A covered tray stood on the cleared dressing table. She removed the napkin, trying not to hope. A large bowl of steaming soup, it looked like chicken-noodle; a plate of mashed potatoes and some very soft-looking meatloaf. A pot of tea. Utensils; paper napkin.

No dentures.

Perhaps—by the bed? She went and looked, but there was nothing new on the bedside table. A faded, flowered flannel gown and blue corduroy robe, not new, lay on the bed itself, which had been turned down for the night. Felt slippers on the floor, new but cheap. Her shoes were gone.

Miss Besserman accepted her loss, and returned to the dressing table. Sitting sideways to her reflection, she began resolutely on the soup. Then the mashed potatoes, and as much of the meatloaf as she could manage—it was rather tiring. She ate steadily, with delicate but purposeful attention: absorbing not indifferent food, but nourishment. Strength; thinking capacity. Perhaps even courage.

Afterwards she lay on the bed and had another try at evoking that lawyer—although she would much prefer to find a way out of her predicament before he came. Without making a public scene. Unfortunately, she found herself becoming a little nauseous—and then, very languid.

Was it a natural reaction, or had they put some drug into her food? Miss Besserman's heart began to beat in dread, at the idea. Was she going to "pass out," become totally helpless?

She forced herself up again and walked around the room, put up the windowblind that would go up and stared out the window; walked some more. A bell rang downstairs; and as if the summons were for her she went and opened her door. In the hall below she could hear the man speaking, but could not make out his words.

With dreamlike new courage she went to the head of the stairs, and saw him standing down there with his back to her, talking on the telephone. Kicking occasionally at a corner of the rug—for variation, scratching his head.

He said, "Well, it's not my fault. Why did she let it go on so long? What's she waiting for, Christmas?"

Then he listened again, and presently said a word which Miss Besserman had never in her life heard pronounced. She absorbed it dully, and went on listening.

"They can always find the money if they have to," he said. "This is no bargain basement, Howie—we've got everything here, you know that. Well, then, let her find a doctor for the same money. Up to her."

He hung up, then bent over and straightened the rug corner, grunting a little. Miss Besserman continued to stand at the head of the stairs even after he disappeared. She was swaying a little; it occurred to her that she might overbalance and fall down the stairs. So she went back into her room. Shut the door, and leaned her forehead against it.

It seemed a long way to the bed. After long consideration, she made it . . . and then discovered that the lamp still burned, far away, on the dressing table.

But later, when she woke briefly, it had gone out.

CHAPTER FIVE

WHATEVER MADE YOU drop off to sleep in your dress, Violet?" Mrs. Kay asked her in the morning. "I'll have to find time to press it. You'd better stay in your robe awhile, it won't matter up here."

Soon her dress lay over Mrs. Kay's arm, a prisoner to that known strength. Miss Besserman put on the robe. She looked at the tray of renewed nourishment, waiting on the dressing table, and knew that she must not touch any of it. The smell of coffee was strong.

She swallowed, and said in a small voice: "When is he coming?"

Mrs. Kay, making the bed, seemed not to hear.

"When is the lawyer coming, Mrs. Kay?"

"As soon as he can make it," Mrs. Kay replied then. This short answer puzzled Miss Besserman, and began to alarm her, until she realized that Mrs. Kay's displeasure was not for herself.

"I told him the longer he waited, the less inclined you'd be to see him at all," Mrs. Kay was going on, snappishly. "After all, he's the one that's asking, you're not the one that wants a change. Right?"

I am not Elva Ryan, Miss Besserman thought fiercely.

Mrs. Kay gave the bed a final slap, and went over to the window.

"You've made a fine mess of this shade," she observed. "Just leave things alone, will you, Violet? I've got enough to do these days, with two of you."

The smell of the coffee she must not touch was fraying Miss Besserman's nerves.

"Well it's your own choice to have two of us, Mrs. Kay," she said tartly.

Mrs. Kay looked around, then finished replacing the rolled shade. When she turned back her tone was milder.

"Get up and eat your breakfast, dear, then I'll come back and help you tidy. You feel like breakfast, don't you?"

"I don't know," said Miss Besserman falsely. Then: "Yes," she said hastily, as Mrs. Kay frowned. She got up and dawdled over retying her robe until Mrs. Kay left her alone again.

Miss Besserman listened, and heard her go downstairs. The poor old lady in the back of the house had already received whatever attention she got; it was these sounds which had awakened Miss Besserman, and to which she had lain apprehensively listening for some time. But there were no cries, or sinister noises—why should there be? It was to their interest to keep her well and alive. The same was true for herself. Probably they were both drugged, but that was all.

For the first time in many years, Miss Besserman felt entire indifference to her appearance—at least so far as her captors were concerned, and she was not likely to see anybody else. Also, her brief exchange with Mrs. Kay this morning had given her a glimpse of some possible balance of power that would not be entirely on Mrs.

36

Kay's side. So, no longer caring how she appeared to them, and not quite so afraid, Miss Besserman planned a small counterattack of her own.

To begin with, she carried the coffee down the hall to the bathroom and disposed of it. The Wheatena made the same journey. Then she left her tray where it was and went downstairs.

They were both in the breakfast room, or whatever it was: the man with the remains of a large breakfast on the table before him, drinking coffee and reading a newspaper; Mrs. Kay doing something in the pantry. At his exclamation she came back into the room with them, and both of them stared at Miss Besserman. (They really were very *sturdy*-looking.)

Then Mrs. Kay said, "What do you want, Miss Besserman?"

It was a tiny satisfaction that she did not say "Violet."

"Am I not allowed to come here?" Miss Besserman asked.

"Certainly, if you like," Mrs. Kay replied, after a small pause. "Only you aren't very tidy yet, are you?"

This cruel remark made no slightest wound; Miss Besserman had faced her Armageddon the night before.

"I won't stay, if it bothers you," she said politely. "But may I have another cup of coffee? I'm afraid I didn't feel strong enough to carry down my tray."

There was another pause. The son looked at his mother, who said: "Of course." She added, "Are you allowed so much coffee?"

"As much as I like," said Miss Besserman.

The pot was on the table—not the pretty china one,

but a large aluminum pot. Mrs. Kay reached down another plastic cup and saucer, and Miss Besserman slipped into the chair farthest from Roddy. There was a plate of toast still on the table.

"I'll just drink it here, if I may," she murmured, to the returning Mrs. Kay. Who said ironically, "Why not?" and then stood beside her, a little to the rear. Roddy continued to send her blank looks, over his newspaper. With restrained eagerness, Miss Besserman received the full cup.

Even black, the first sip was delicious. Under their silent regard, she drank as much, and as quickly, as she could. It was a little unnerving. Did they expect her to keel over, as she had last night? Miss Besserman suspected there had been less of whatever-it-was in her breakfast, since she might after all have to be produced conscious sometime during the day. But to reassure them (and break the silence) she gave a tiny yawn.

"I can't seem to wake up," she explained. "I think it might help to have something solid to eat, if I may. Aren't my dentures ready yet, uh, Roddy?"

His head jerked up. He gave her one long stare so unfriendly that she looked away, afraid she had somehow exceeded her license.

Then—and she could hear his beginning grin—he decided to answer.

"Why, I guess you better gum it awhile longer, Aunt Elva," he said.

His mother hardly let him finish.

"Now, Roddy—it's no joke. No, they're not ready," she said to Miss Besserman. "It's a shame, but it seems like ordinary glue doesn't work on that stuff. Roddy's going out and get the right kind as soon as he's done. *Are you done?*" she asked him.

He began to fold up his paper, still good-humored.

"Looks like it."

"And may I ask about my coiffure?" Miss Besserman persisted.

Mrs. Kay was ready for her.

"Why, I had to send that out to be cleaned—that's too nice a piece to have Roddy scrubbing at it, I'm sure you aren't supposed to wash an expensive wig like that at home, now are you?"

"No," said Miss Besserman agreeably. And without surprise. Absently, she poured herself more coffee; and in a delicate gesture lifted a piece of the toast.

"May I?"

"Sure. Live it up," said Roddy.

He got up and stretched, then strolled away through the pantry to some unimaginable destination. Miss Besserman did not think he was going to buy any glue.

His mother decided to make some apology for him.

"He's upset about this," she said. "About what we have to do. Well, we all are—people shouldn't be forced into such a position through no fault of their own. It's a strain on us all. We just have to remember it won't last more than a few days, isn't that right?"

Miss Besserman, shamelessly consuming what might be her last meal for some time, gave an absent nod in reply. Mrs. Kay began to show irritation.

"Don't overload your stomach, Violet," she said. "We'd better go up now, and see what we can do to straighten you out. You wouldn't want anybody to come and catch you looking like that, would you?"

No bruise appeared upon Miss Besserman's feelings. Her vanity seemed to have died. It was an almost exhilarating release.

"What would our penalty be, if we were caught?" she inquired mildly, taking the last piece of toast.

"Caught!" Mrs. Kay echoed. Her expression altered. She fixed a more threatening look upon Miss Besserman, who was pouring herself the last of the coffee. "What put an idea like that into your head?",

"Well, it's natural isn't it? After all, I'm not Mrs. Ryan. I haven't any right to keep this house from—from whoever wants it. And I suppose it's valuable, or they wouldn't want it."

"Now you listen to me, Miss Besserman. The people who haven't any *right* are the people who are trying to take this place away! And from a helpless old lady, too. You just be good and clear about that. You're only speaking up for someone that can't speak up for herself, and that's got every right in this world on her side ! Just remember that," Mrs. Kay said with slow emphasis. "And don't forget you're protecting your own interests, too. Why, you wouldn't have taken that place without the view, would you?"

Everything was gone. Miss Besserman felt much stronger. She did need a napkin, though, and none was apparent.

"I wonder if I might have a napkin?" she murmured.

Mrs. Kay showed a sudden capacity for temper.

"Miss Besserman, you asked me a foolish question,

40

and I'm doing my best to give you a sensible answer. Are you listening to me, or not?"

Miss Besserman shrank back, instantly intimidated.

"Oh . . . oh, yes . . ."

"Then please stop making things harder than they have to be, will you? You've already frightened poor Mrs. Ryan out of her wits—and caused so much damage Roddy's running his legs off, trying to repair it—and now you come wandering around down here, acting like you're ten years old and not very bright at that! Don't you think it's time you pulled yourself together and acted like the lady you're supposed to be? Don't you?"

(Her temper was no longer real; she was only bullying now. But, realizing this, Miss Besserman still shrank from the sound of it.)

She whispered, "I'm sorry, I—didn't mean to upset you—"

Mrs. Kay glared a moment longer, and then showed that she relented.

"Well," she said. "I don't suppose you did. And I didn't mean to fly off the handle. Let's forget it, and go upstairs and fix you up nice. All you have to remember," she said, rising and leaning impressively over the table, "is that you haven't a thing in the world to worry about. You're doing the right thing—for yourself, and for Mrs. Ryan too—and I'll be with you every minute when that lawyer comes, I'll see that he watches his step good, don't think I won't. We don't have to take a thing from those Ryans, they haven't got a leg to stand on legally. Talk about 'penalties'!" she finished, scornful.

Miss Besserman had no intention of talking about

penalties any more. She smiled weakly, covering her mouth. Mrs. Kay lost interest in her.

"I think I'll press that dress, first," she murmured, beginning to clear the table. "It's a little young, but I can find a nice white scarf, or shawl or something, to cover the top. And put a rug over your legs. Why don't you go on up and rest till I come? Think you can make it back up by yourself?"

"Oh, yes. Yes."

She was obediently scrambling up from her chair, Mrs. Kay was carrying dishes into the pantry, when a loud, grinding bell-sound rang through the house. Both women stopped dead.

"Roddy!" called Mrs. Kay.

She turned to her guest, demonstrably calm.

"Now that can't be anyone, this time of morning, but you'd better just . . . Roddy, help Violet upstairs, will you? I'll answer."

He had appeared at a lope, heavy and quick-eyed. Even at that moment Miss Besserman noted unhappily that Roddy would be the one to lose his head if anything went really wrong. Perhaps dangerously so. He came for her now without a word, as if she were a parcel. Miss Besserman shut her eyes.

But his mother's voice said: "Careful, son"; and Miss Besserman felt herself half-lifted around the table and out of the room without any pain. Daring to look again, she received a fast, confused view of the pantry, of a long, old-fashioned kitchen, and then was thrust up the darkness of a stairwell. The enclosure was brief; they soon came out on the landing which joined the front stairs. She caught a glimpse of the front door, even of the figure standing outside—so distorted by beveled glass and her own vision that it might have been anything waiting to come in.

Whoever it was was no more than twenty feet away—near enough to cry out to. Miss Besserman had neither time nor impulse for such a cry. Nor even the intention. The panic of flight was on her too; and the breathy man at her side had become a kind of ally, helping her scramble away into hiding.

CHAPTER SIX

It was the kind of place you felt you ought to remember, whether any real memory was possible or not.

So far as Tony Ryan knew, he had never stood on this sloping porch before in his life, trying to peer through the cut-glass door. He thought he would at least have remembered all the vines—it was like being in a jungle hideout. But if he had ever been brought here it was many years ago. His grandfather had died when he was six years old; perhaps the place had looked different then.

Time was passing. He gave the bell another turn, trying again to peer in, and this time he was able to make out a large, fractured shadow-shape looming toward him. The door opened partly, and a woman stood in the aperture. A large, fractured woman-shape, as a matter of fact.

He smiled at her. Why not?

Her only response was to say: "Yes?" Not a welcoming sound.

"Mrs. Ryan?"

He supposed it was possible. He had thought he was coming to see an old lady; but his step-grandmother (or whatever she was) had been no part of the lore of his growing up. If his grandfather had taken a child-second-bride, he supposed this could be it.

But the woman replied: "Mrs. Ryan isn't down yet. Who's calling, please?"

"Well, I'm Anthony Ryan. Could I see her? I don't mind waiting."

She didn't quite know what to do with this. The door stayed as it was.

"Well," she said finally, "we expected some notice, Mr. Ryan. It would be better if you came with an appointment. Mrs. Ryan is elderly."

"I thought she would be," he said, relieved. After a pause he saw that she could find no answer to this—naturally—so he added more.

"Just tell her it's a grandson," he said, tactfully vague. "Anthony. Tony."

Now she was looking him over—with special attention for the Crimson Glory he had brought along for the old lady and stuck in his pocket, head out, while he was driving. It seemed to be still there; but doing no harm. Certainly not meriting that sort of look.

In a small rise of impatience, he asked: "Look—is she all right?"

"Certainly she's all right," the woman replied quickly; and did at last open the door wider. She still didn't move to let him in, though. "It's just that we were —Mrs. Ryan was expecting the family's legal representative. We did not expect a member of the family, Mr. Ryan."

"Well," he said, acknowledging the point, "I suppose not. Look, why don't you— Are you a relation of hers, or something?"

Unexpectedly, she produced a smile. Not the kind you answered, more for looking at. He looked at it, serious, and missed some words she was saying.

"What?"

"I said, won't you come in, Mr. Ryan?"

"Yes, of course. Thank you."

The hallway really stunned him—that, and the glimpse of the room beyond. Such old, old, spotty-mirror tranquillity, surely it matched no living memories of anybody? It stirred no memory in him—only a sense of loss, far down in his heart, and he didn't know why. Whatever it represented was so *gone*.

The woman watched him, still smiling.

"Memories?" she suggested.

"No, not really. It's been too long for that."

"Surely you remember Mrs. Ryan?"

"Probably not," he said, regretful. "I'm not sure we ever came across each other—if we did, I was awfully small. She may not even know who I am. I'd like to say hello to her, though."

"Well," said the woman, "I don't see why you shouldn't, if you don't mind waiting a while. As long as you haven't come to upset the poor soul. May I ask if you had some reason for coming today, Mr. Ryan?"

He had begun to have enough of this one, whoever she was.

"Just tell her I'd like to pay my respects, that's all. If she's up to it. Is she an invalid?"

"Certainly not. Mrs. Ryan is getting along, that's all, and she leads a very quiet life. But she's in good health, and her mind is perfectly clear. I'll just go and ask her," she said with new decisiveness, "if she'd like to come down. You won't mind a little wait?"

"No, no."

"You can wait right in here. Probably you'll enjoy having a look through your grandfather's books—he was a great reader, wasn't he? I'll turn the lamp on for you, it's a little dark in here."

She did this, reaching a sturdy hand through deep fringe to produce a smothered gleam. Useless; not even ornamental. And somehow depressing. He turned it off again when he was alone, and the fringe felt like palpable dust stroking his hand. He stood rubbing his ghost-touched skin, listening to various creaks and steps overhead. The rooms around him waited like museum rooms —some little country museum, open maybe one day a week. Or just if anyone wanted to see it.

Silently he began to wander: through the parlor, back through a heavily furnished, dead dining room, into a small sort of garden-room place that looked, at last, as if people still came here.

But no one he could imagine. He ran his fingers absently over the coffee-ringed oilcloth on the table, stared out into a crowd of discouraged bushes and vines through dull panes. If those scandalous lovers of forty years ago had sat together here, any souvenir of their presence was lost. Or had they been sad lovers?

He didn't want to think so. The grandfather whom, it was sometimes ominously suggested, he resembled had escaped from the family silver-chest and stayed out. More than he himself had yet managed. He would have liked to think this defiance had been successful. But from the look of things, the old boy had jumped his felt-lined box only to tarnish in another dim enclosure.

Too bad.

Someone came heavily down the stairs. He turned and wandered back, but the descending person did not appear in the front hall after all, and his waiting continued. He put idle fingers on the closed sliding doors, and found they did not respond. Stuck, or locked?

He hunkered down to see. The rose fell from his pocket and he picked it up and stuck it between his teeth, presently got out his penknife and picked tranquilly at a brass catch which seemed to hold the two doors together. When they parted he rose and slid through, and found himself in his grandfather's consulting room.

Must be. Big desk full of cubbyholes, sturdy wooden chairs, diplomas hanging on the walls. He went over and read, twirling the rose. Still legible; still true: Mortimer John Ryan, 1908, The College of Medicine, the University of . . . *Iowa?*

He stared around the plain room again. Iowa . . . he was partly descended from an Iowan! It sounded like an Indian, he wished it were. He ran an affectionate hand over the desk, then thought to wipe his hand. But it held no dust. In new interest, he opened a door to explore further.

Examination room. Everything looked very high—cabinets, cases, the torture table itself. Think of those little creatures in long skirts hopping up there . . . Except that in the twenties, their skirts were as short as now. He fiddled absently, found the stirrups tucked beneath the table's edge, and was extending one, when commotion behind him made him turn.

"What in *hell*—!" a man's voice exclaimed.

A big one. Somewhere in his thirties; flabby; sweating about something. And standing still after his outburst. Making an effort.

"Hello," said Tony, mildly.

"You're not supposed to be in here, Ryan," he said, after a pause.

"Why not?"

Couldn't think why not. Stood back, gesturing, instead. The gesture said, Out; but neither of them moved.

"You live here too?" Tony said politely.

"Look," said the citizen, beginning over. "You better come out now. This is supposed to be locked up. There's a local doctor uses it sometimes."

"Oh?" Tony began, carefully, to work the stirrup back. "Pays rent, I hope?"

The silence extended. Then suddenly broke.

"She can use any extra income she can get—you know how she's fixed. Come on, let's go."

A pleasant warmth began to rise inside Tony. He made a delicate readjustment of the second stirrup, watching the other as he did so.

"I don't know how she's, uh, fixed. Just that she lives here, and seems to have plenty of company. You a relative?"

"That's right. . . . Look, you want to come out now? I think she's coming downstairs."

No one was coming down; they would have heard.

But a voice was calling from upstairs.

"Roddy! Roddy?"

Tony smiled. The man looked at him with eyes like petrified prunes.

"Come on, let's *go*," he said, ugly then.

"After you, Roddy."

It took a minute of hard deciding, but apparently he had to answer.

When he had gone there was no further reason to stay. Some long intervention had clearly come between his grandfather's leaving these rooms and his own coming here at last. They were just old rooms, now.

But it was funny she hadn't sold the stuff. Or was it salable?

He didn't know. He went back and got his rose, fallen to the floor from somebody's desk. He hadn't seen anybody yet he would have given it to.

Upstairs, in a rage, Roddy breathed at his mother:

"That damned kooky kid's into the doc's place—didn't you lock it?"

"Yes." She looked at him, was thoughtful. "Well, what difference does it make? Roddy, you'll have to get her teeth. She won't budge without them."

"I told him she rented it part-time to a local doc. He picked that lock!"

"All right. I don't care. Get the teeth, Roddy."

But he stood in angry indecision, sweating still.

"I think this is a waste of time. What the hell difference does it make, what that snotty kid thinks? Nobody sent him here. He's just snooping!"

"All right. He'll still go back and talk about what he sees. Besides, it's good practice—I want to see how she behaves. Go get the teeth, Roddy."

He muttered, "I didn't have time to do anything to them yet—I don't know how to get one out without cracking the whole damn thing."

"That's all right. I'll tell her you fixed them but it might not stay. That will make her watch her talking, too."

"I still think it's a waste of time," he grumbled. But he went, quieted down, toward his own room. She called softly after him: "Stay up here with Elva, will you, dear? Just so she doesn't get lively, or whatever."

He didn't reply. But she knew he had heard, and would do as she asked.

CHAPTER SEVEN

Miss besserman had never been so frightened in her life.

The terrors and humiliations behind her seemed to count for nothing, compared to what she was about to do. For up to now she had only feared *outwardly,* so to speak. Feared these large, strange people who kept her here, deprived her of parts of her person and—perhaps worst of all—suggested a cruel roughness which she could not imagine, and yet which she did not doubt existed.

Still, her essential self had so far remained beyond their reach. Now she was about to yield it up. In craven consent, she was going down to cheat and lie to *an ordinary person like herself*—for even if she stuck to her first resolve and said nothing, her silence would consent to what Mrs. Kay said for her. How had she ever come so far, down so dark a path?

For Miss Besserman did not deceive herself, she was already on that path. She had already cooperated by letting herself be "tidied up" for her old-lady role—and had even used her compliance to get back her teeth! Well, now she had her teeth. (Though damaged, they said. And with no adhesive.) But she had probably paid for them with her soul.

Vanity. Cowardice and vanity had defeated her. So long as she looked like this she could not bear to insist that she was Violet Besserman. It wasn't even a matter of being believed; she knew now that she might very well *deny* this was Violet Besserman, if anyone guessed!

Shut in that upstairs bedroom, with Mrs. Kay brushing and powdering and soothing her, she had simply withdrawn into despairing consent. This was the only way, this dreadful interval, of regaining her true self. Her freedom, and her home. (Her view she no longer thought of. At this price, it could never comfort her again.) Afterwards, she could creep back home and put her shattered self together again.

Behind the closed bedroom door she had thought this way. If you could call it thinking. But when she found herself outside that door, being guided far too rapidly toward the real person waiting downstairs, her coma ended. She understood what it was that she was about to do.

And it was too late.

Her strength failed her. Abruptly, she slid downward from her hostess's hand, so rapidly that both of them almost tumbled down. Mrs. Kay's reflexes were quick and strong, however. Before her knees met the floor Miss Besserman was yanked upright again and pinned against the stair railings. It was breathlessly painful.

It was also silent. Mrs. Kay took a moment to control her breathing, so that her ominous voice carried no further than Miss Besserman's ear.

"Now no more of that. *Understand?*"

Miss Besserman nodded, dumb.

"Now stand up, and behave yourself."

"I couldn't help it—"

"You can help it. Stand up!"

Miss Besserman, left alone on the railing, pushed herself shakily upright. This time Mrs. Kay took a hard grasp on her arm.

Her voice suddenly rang out at normal volume—deafening, after the whispers.

"All right, Elva, let's go down now. You've got a nice surprise coming, worth getting up early for. You'll see."

Miss Besserman shuffled rapidly around the newel post and put one felt slipper out. Her thoughts had scattered like birds to a sound of gunshot.

"That's right. Got hold of the railing? That's right. You ought to have one of those little stair elevators, you'd come down a lot more if you did. That's something you could really use, isn't it?"

Because of all this noise, someone came into the hallway below and stood waiting for them. Miss Besserman didn't even try to look until she had got all the way down, quite fast. Then she stood still, clutching the post. Her heart beat wildly. Somebody very tall was coming up to her.

"Aunt Elva?"

A new voice. A young voice. Someone free, from outside. Why had he come in here?

"All right if I call you Aunt Elva? I don't know what else—unless you're Mrs. Ryan to me, I hope not."

She still could not get him into focus; but, desperate with confusion, she went on peering upward.

"Not Mrs. Ryan. . . ."

The words burst from her, beyond recall.

Somebody laughed.

"Okay. Aunt Elva it is, then. And I'm Tony. That you probably never heard of?"

Why was he smiling? For she suddenly saw him—stood and stared up at him, as at a focal point around which the whirling world might settle.

A young man. Very tall and thin, and smiling. Lovely teeth. Lovely soft dark hair, brushed back long like the young men in portraits of long ago. Was he dressed up too, like herself?

She suspected her own confusion; and yet clung to it, with nothing else she dared cling to. He was no more real than she, in his strange beauty. He was pretending too.

She took the hand which, she saw, he was holding out to her. It closed around hers with a shock of warmth that made her cry out faintly.

"Oh—"

"Aunt Elva? You all right?"

Mrs. Kay's brisk voice fell between them.

"She's fine. Just a bit overcome, aren't you, dear? Come in and sit down now, you'll be fine."

She could not hold on to him, he moved back for Mrs. Kay's authority, and she was ironly helped away from him.

But he came after.

When Mrs. Kay had put her into a chair, he stood in front of it, and put a rose into her lap.

"I peeled off the thorns," he said. "It won't bite."

She sat looking down at it. It was a real rose, a home

55

rose, such as she not held since her sister had been alive and kept their garden. She put her fingers upon the satiny underside of the petals, looked into its tilted deep-red heart.

"Crimson Glory?" she said to it, wondering. "What a nice one. . . ." Her sibilants whistled, recalling her to silence. She did not look up to thank him, as she had meant to do.

Mrs. Kay said for her, "That was very nice of you, Mr. Ryan, and I'm sure she appreciates it. Her garden meant a lot to her—still does, though we can't afford to keep it up."

He hunkered down beside the chair, so that she could see him out of the corner of her eye.

"You've kept Grandfather's room all these years," he said to her. "His diplomas, and everything. Do you know, I never knew he came from Iowa. I don't think I know much about him at all, really. Do you like to talk about him?"

"Well, not just yet, perhaps," Mrs. Kay's voice said overhead. "Maybe just getting acquainted is enough, this time. You're the first of them that's been near her in all these years, you know."

He stood up again. Standing, his voice sounded quite different.

"Look, I may be a Ryan, but I'm harmless. Do you have to stay with her? She looks fine."

"She is fine," said Mrs. Kay's voice, sharper too. "She's fine because she has good care, in her own home, and no one is allowed to pester her about giving it up. If you really want to show some interest in her, you might remind your family about that, Mr. Ryan. That would be the best way you could help her, and I'll tell you so frankly. She'd tell you the same, if she wasn't too polite."

Miss Besserman covered her rose with a trembling hand, and continued to look down. There was, overhead, what seemed an unbearably long pause.

Then his voice said, faraway: "You didn't tell me your name."

"I'm Mrs. Kay," she said promptly, "and Mrs. Ryan and I have shared this home together for many years, because that was the only way she could afford to stay here. Maybe you don't know it, but she was left with very little besides the tenancy—the *lifelong* tenancy of this house. That's just about all she has—that, and us, Mr. Ryan."

There was another terrible pause.

Then he came down again, beside her.

"Aunt Elva?"

She made herself face him, a kind of mute apology. He looked at her awhile, but very gently, so that she forgot to keep her lips pressed together.

"Thank you . . . ," she risked saying, at last. But no more.

He answered seriously, "I don't know why things were like that, Aunt Elva. I'm sorry they were—honestly. I hope they weren't too bad. Were they? Are they?"

"We're perfectly all right, Mr. Ryan," the voice above them broke in, "and we'll continue to be. *If* we're not interfered with. That's all we ask, and all we've ever asked, and your family should understand that by now."

He had shut his eyes while the talking lasted, and she

57

looked at the lashes, the strong dark brows, in a wonder of pleasure. When he opened his eyes again she could see how *new* they looked, the way young eyes did, as if they had just been made—hardly used at all. But no young eyes had looked at her this way before.

He began to smile, catching her at her examination.

"Well, what if I come back another time, Aunt Elva?" he said, as if he had been deciding something. "I'll give you some notice, and you can tell me what's a good time for you. Is that better?"

"Yes," she whispered.

Mrs. Kay did not speak, or move.

"Bring you some Queen Elizabeth next time—how about that? What other kinds do you like? Maybe we've got them—I don't know all the names."

She shook her head, smiling a little too but not risking any more esses. He put his hand over hers and pressed lightly. Then he got up.

His altered voice said, "Right—here I go, Madam K. Thanks so very much. Give you a hand up, Aunt Elva?"

She didn't need to answer, of course; Mrs. Kay was refusing for her. But she did look after him, and he waved from the hall, and smiled at her.

Even after the door closed she could hear him on the porch, then on the steps. But on the sidewalk, after the first crisp steps, she did not know which steps were his, and so lost him.

No one came back for her. Mrs. Kay had gone directly upstairs and she could hear them talking up there, their voices sounding emphatic and rather loud. She could not distinguish any words.

Presently it occurred to her that there was nothing to stop her from leaving the house. She could get up and be at the front door, out in the street, in only a few moments. Only a short walk along the sidewalk would bring her to the apartment-house entrance. Aside from the felt slippers, she was presentable. She had her teeth.

Yet she did nothing. She only sat on, exhausted and bemused, as if she were indeed Aunt Elva reliving an unexpected visit. Turning the rose over slowly in her lap, and waiting.

CHAPTER EIGHT

She's like a prisoner in that house," Tony Ryan said to his mother. "I don't think she was afraid of me at all. She's just generally intimidated. That woman never lets her get a word in."

"Well, they've lived together for years, apparently," she replied. "Whatever the relationship is, it must suit her."

She sat at the card table, in a welter of envelopes being addressed for the League of Women Voters, but she scrupulously stopped writing whenever he spoke to her. Besides, she liked to look at him. She privately thought his Pilgrim-style hair very becoming; and no one could say he didn't keep himself clean.

But she could not help saying, "Those shoes are getting a little tacky, dear."

They were actually sandals. This was what she meant. He didn't hear her.

"I don't think it suits her. Maybe it never did, maybe she had to take whoever she could get. Is it true she doesn't have anything except the house? Or the use of the house?"

"I don't know, dear. I don't think we ever knew much about her. She isn't really family, you know, Tony."

"She's a human being," he said. "And a Ryan too, legally."

"Well, ask your father," she replied, beginning again to write. "He may know more about it."

"I doubt if he does. I think Grannie clamped down on that subject years ago. Do you suppose he'd mind if I went in and talked to Mr. Bingham about it? After all, it's our property. Someday."

"I just don't know, Tony. Ask him."

"Well, I thought of going by this afternoon. To Bingham and Whatsit, I mean."

She put down her pen again.

"Goodness, what's the hurry? And how have you got so much loose time, anyway?"

"I haven't," he said, and grinned as he got up. "But that old girl looks as if she's got even less. I'd like to know how things really are with her."

His mother looked at him thoughtfully, but refrained from comment. The children had been brought up to accept social responsibility; there was no real reason to interfere that she could see, if Tony wished to take an interest in his grandfather's widow.

So she said only, "You'd better telephone Mr. Bingham first, you know"; and went on with her envelopes.

His grandmother's—and father's—lawyer was in downtown Boston, the senior partner in a small, old firm which prided itself on being both. Mr. Bingham Senior was Tony's bird. With impartial cordiality, he gave Tony a late-afternoon appointment; and when they met, in his quiet office, seemed pleased to catch up on the last fifteen years or so. He gave Tony an eerie feeling that his grandmother might still be alive and well, somewhere on the premises; the old lady he had seen that morning took on aspects of mirage.

It seemed safer to begin with the question of property, after they had covered Harvard Today and Yesterday and come to a stop.

"I went by and had a look at Grandfather's house this morning," he said. "While it's still there. Everything's pretty much as he left it, it seems."

Mr. Bingham was interested to hear this. He shook his head over the decay of the town in general.

"Some of these old New England towns have had a hard time of it," he said sadly. "They've had to wait for the whole pattern of the country to change, in order to begin to come back to life. A sad experience to go through them nowadays; I avoid it myself, when I can."

"I don't really understand how we're able to sell the place while, uh, Aunt Elva's still living in it," Tony said. "What's supposed to become of her?"

Mr. Bingham's eyebrows went up, a fraction.

"You know the lady, do you?"

"Met her this morning. She declined the 'Mrs. Ryan' bit—being tactful, maybe. But a less scandalous old body I never saw, Mr. Bingham."

"I never met your grandfather's second wife, myself," he replied, with mild interest. "Not a Boston woman, though, I believe. Wasn't she from the Western states somewhere too?"

"Was she? I didn't even know that Grandfather came from Iowa, until I saw his diploma this morning."

"You seem to have had quite an interesting experience, Tony."

His tone was slightly wistful. Apparently in this pre-servative air old scandals did not die. He seemed to wait, for further details which did not come—since Tony had none to offer. Then he murmured, "Of course, I remember your grandfather quite well. He had something of your build and coloring, you know."

"So they tell me."

"Shorter hair, though," said Mr. Bingham dryly.

"I suppose so. In the twenties, wasn't it?"

They regarded each other gravely.

Mr. Bingham sighed, and said: "Now you want me to explain this business of the lifelong occupancy, do you? I've discussed it with your father, you know—there's nothing to worry about there."

"For whom, Mr. Bingham?" Tony asked.

He got a glance of mild severity.

"I don't know how much of the background you're aware of. It's quite simple. Your grandmother had inherited considerable property, including the house in Lincoln where you still live, and this of course belonged absolutely to her. It was only necessary to secure whatever property your grandfather might have to his children's inheritance—and that turned out to be, simply, the house you saw this morning."

"What if there'd been more children, though?" Tony inquired. "There weren't, were there?"

"No, no—they weren't a young couple, you know. Past forty, both of them."

"In the *twenties?*"

Mr. Bingham quashed this naïveté.

"Of this century; yes."

"I meant, she didn't look that old," said Tony, off balance.

Mr. Bingham was tolerant.

"Eighty-odd, I believe."

"Is she? Well, she seems very much alive, Mr. Bingham. I don't think she's used up her lifelong occupancy yet."

"I hope not," he said politely. "And I'm glad to hear that she'll be able to enjoy the new place. I gather the old one is in pretty poor repair. You're concerned about her, are you?"

"I wondered what the position was . . . The woman who lives with her says the house is all she has."

"Ah, that lady. You met her, did you? Is she some sort of relative? She seems to handle all Mrs. Ryan's affairs for her—says there's some physical handicap, I believe."

"She told me Aunt Elva's eyesight was poor. But she knows a Crimson Glory when she sees it."

"Good for her."

"I don't think there's any relationship. They just seem to share the house. Her version is that Aunt Elva is being thrown out on the street."

"Oh, nonsense, Tony. She'll simply be exchanging rather dilapidated quarters for rather better ones. Her lifetime tenancy of the Brook Street property," Mr. Bingham said with exactitude, "is in no way being interfered with. Naturally, she'll be accommodated during the interim."

"What interim?"

"While the house comes down and the apartment goes up," said Mr. Bingham in plain English. "As for her having nothing else, I doubt that very much. I'm sure your grandfather made other provision for her. I

64

shouldn't listen to this companion, or whatever she is, if I were you—we learned to disregard her letters quite some time ago. She seemed to feel that every sort of repair was our responsibility—which of course has no basis whatsoever in fact. Mrs. Ryan herself understood this; we never had such letters from her. That was why I assumed that she was, um, failing."

Tony was silent awhile, and Mr. Bingham allowed him to be.

He said finally, "Well, I thought you might know what her circumstances are. And more about this crew that lives with her."

"Is it a crew?"

"Well, there's a grown son of Mrs. Kay's, too. They're pretty rough people. But they seem to be all she has. What if she isn't able to live alone? Or what if she's attached to the old place? Hasn't she any say about what happens? Hasn't she got to agree to the change, or sign something? Mrs. Kay seems to think so."

"My dear Tony, certainly not. I should never have let your family's property be tied up in such a way. It's been enough of a loss to you as it is—the taxes have been your responsibility all these years, you know. You are entitled to take this opportunity now that it's come up. You have done more than enough," he said emphatically, "for a lady who, after all, has no claim on you whatsoever. I thought at the time that your grandmother was generous in agreeing to these terms, and I told her so. But she wanted it this way and so I had no choice."

"You're not going down to see the old lady at all?"

"No reason in the world to—and, I must admit, I have

no desire to meet this Mrs. Kay, after enduring all her letters." He added, "There is a local attorney we sometimes employ who can help make the arrangements for Mrs. Ryan when the time comes. Will that make you feel better?"

"Oh, I feel fine, thanks. Just wondered. It was a funny situation to walk into, cold. I only went to see the house . . . pay respects. . . ."

"Of course," Mr. Bingham agreed. "Well, I really shouldn't get personally involved, if I were you—and if you don't mind having an opinion. It's an odd situation, and it's always been delicate, but it seems to have worked itself out well enough. Your grandparents both behaved very well, the second Mrs. Ryan has never given any trouble, and she will probably be quite relieved to find herself in a fine new place in her declining years. As for these people she's been living with—it is probably they who are making the objections, and that is hardly our concern, is it?"

"I think they're making some shady use of Grandfather's offices. Renting them out part-time to a quack, or something fishy."

"Well, that will soon come to an end, if so, won't it? The whole situation sounds very untidy, Tony, and I repeat that I hope you will not involve yourself—or your family—in it. However, I'm very glad you had a chance to see your grandfather's house while it is still there—one likes to fill in these gaps while there is still time. It isn't often that young people realize this, I congratulate you. And thank you so much for telling me about it, very thoughtful of you, Tony."

Going out—flushed out, so to speak, on this wave of cordiality—Tony clung momentarily to a doorframe.

"Is all this going to happen soon, Mr. Bingham?"

"Oh, quite soon, I think. We've just about completed our negotiations, and I expect the company will want to move ahead with their building as soon as they can. If there are any of your grandfather's things you would like to have, why don't you let me speak to Mr. Bailey about it? That's the local attorney I mentioned, he'll be seeing Mrs. Ryan in any case, it can be easily handled."

And don't go near the water.

Tony said Thanks, it was an idea; he would let Mr. Bingham know. They parted, with wary goodwill.

CHAPTER NINE

Someone came to the house that night. Miss Besserman was locked in her room.

She was too drowsy to feel more than a dull alarm when she discovered this, since she had knowingly, sadly, eaten up the oblivion-making food Mrs. Kay brought to her. One could not go on flushing soups and puddings down the lavatory indefinitely, and live. Besides, the night lay ahead of her inescapable and long. She might as well sleep through it.

That morning's bemusement had not lasted. A telephone call had brought Roddy downstairs again soon after young Mr. Ryan had left, when Miss Besserman was discovered and hustled back to her room as if she were an eavesdropper. In fact, she neither understood nor cared to know about Roddy's business dealings. She supposed that was what it was. He had been arguing more money with someone who had finally agreed to pay him three hundred dollars. For what, Miss Besserman could not imagine. With dreary indifference, she faced the fact that it was probably something stolen.

If so, his dishonesty was no worse than hers. What damage she had done that morning to a young man's inheritance only the Lord knew. And could forgive. Miss Besserman was in no spirit to forgive herself. Not even cowardice could be her excuse this time, she had forgotten to be afraid.

Because he had been so unexpectedly, wonderfully kind to her. And she had lost her head.

She had *willingly* and without coercion pretended to be Elva Ryan so that his respectful and loving kindness would not end. So that her heart would go on being taken by this heavenly surprise.

That was the truth of what she had done. Miss Besserman faced it at last, lying still on the strange bed in her locked room, only half-mistress of her mind by now.

All afternoon she had tried to evade the truth—refusing her lunch, refusing to rest, refusing to acknowledge her guilt. What else could I have done? she argued with herself.

She knew very well what else she could have done.

The young were no novelty to her. They were, in fact, Miss Besserman's specialty in her selling days. Everyone had acknowledged how good she was with young people, laughing and joking and never taking offense with their young ways, or losing patience. She had always been lively herself, she liked their liveliness—and how were you going to stay young if you didn't like youth? She *did* like them . . . and they liked her. Even if they did laugh. Why not? Young people laughed at everything. She laughed right with them.

But nothing like this had ever happened before. This gentle offer of affection, to the old lady she pretended to be.

That she was.

Violet Besserman was an old lady too. Seventy-six.

69

But she wasn't Elva Ryan. Never, never again must she pretend to be Elva Ryan.

She lay very still—exhausted; cleansed. Resolve gathered muddily in her mind. She would leave here, however she could, as soon as she could. So that fear and confusion would never make her betray herself again . . . and the young man. When the lawyer came, they must have no one to produce.

She thought, In the morning I will go down and . . . by the front door, and . . . when they, when the . . .

Someone was screaming. Or had screamed?

Ready fear pounced on her again and she lay rigid, staring to hear again whatever poor creature it was, out there in the night.

Only . . . not outside. Somewhere downstairs. And not screaming now, but giving dreadful loud sobbing cries.

Then nothing. Silence.

And silence.

A long while went by, in which Miss Besserman felt herself slowly imprisoned by a waking and helpless sleep. No more sounds reached her; she saw only the unmoving shadows of this room. No part of her moved, or seemed capable of movement.

Was she awake, or caught in a nightmare?

A car started up, in the street below.

That real sound, loud in the unreal quiet, replaced her in the living world. The power to move returned to her, and she caught at the bedclothes—pulled herself sideways in the bed and dizzily hung there.

Somewhere beneath her, sliding doors rumbled—a sound she had long ago known very well. The only closed sliding doors here led to Dr. Ryan's offices—what were they doing in there?

Now came a confusion of footsteps, the mumble of voices. People were downstairs, in the hall. Several people. It was no dream.

Miss Besserman rolled herself off the bed, staggered into motion on the felt slippers she seemed always now to wear, and made for the door. It would not open. She gave it up and tacked around, back to the window, where she could look over the porch roof and see, by the light of the street-lamp, a portion of street and sidewalk between the trees.

The car was still there, engine still running. The people she had heard were coming out to it, their confused and somehow dragging steps sounded on the porch beneath. Swaying, braced against the windowframe, Miss Besserman stared down. The car door opened and its interior came alight, shedding light around it. A huddled group appeared and hung around the open car door; a girl was thrust inside. A girl who gave one cry, quickly silenced as the car door was slammed.

The people left on the sidewalk stood back, and became only two. A man and a woman. Separately they turned, and disappeared beneath the porch roof. The car was driving away, and Miss Besserman watched its red taillights gleam through the leaves, and vanish. The street returned to its night-time desertion.

But she could hear them in the downstairs hall now—Mrs. Kay and her son. Closing and chaining the door, talking in low voices, walking away to some other part of the house.

Miss Besserman crept back to the bed and groped to reenter it—dress and all, slippers and all. She had begun to shake with cold—or with some icy distress her mind would not define. Cold—freezing cold—gripped and shook her in deathly urgency. She had only the sense left in her to crawl and burrow for warmth into the bed and lie there, doubled, bone pressed upon bone, until some return of living warmth relieved her of consciousness.

CHAPTER TEN

THE KEY TURNED in the lock, and Mrs. Kay pushed the door open.

Roddy passed her, carrying a tray. Moving heavily, he put this on the dressing table and gave a hitch to the tie of his soiled robe. He glanced toward the bed, but not as if it contained anyone.

His mother said hoarsely, "I'll be down in a minute. Get dressed."

He padded out without reply.

Mrs. Kay came over to the bed and stood looking down at Miss Besserman, whose eyes were open. She took hold of the covers and threw them back, exposing the rumpled dress and felt slippers, and her puffy face crumpled in disgust.

"Now you've got to stop this, Violet," she said roughly. "Or else you can put on your nightdress and stay in it. Do you hear?"

She was in a bad temper, like her son. Their heavy faces were alike in pallor and puffiness, with dulled dark eyes. When Miss Besserman omitted to answer, she was taken by the arm and pulled upright in bed.

"Now get up. Eat your breakfast. Here, give me your hand."

A little less roughly, Miss Besserman was pulled to her

feet and started toward the dressing table. It seemed an enormous distance; momentum carried her only partway. She wavered to a stop. Mrs. Kay had not begun making the bed, but was standing to watch her. Looking uncertainly back, Miss Besserman discovered this and forced herself the rest of the way.

The coffee and cereal waited there, steaming and unwelcome. Full of new drugs. Her head still felt as if it were stuffed with cotton . . . and with horror. Stupefied, she tried to avoid inhaling the warm scents rising to her—heard a small retching sound escape her lips, and turned away.

Mrs. Kay came up behind and caught her around the waist, pushed her over to the velvet settee.

"You'd better sit there a minute. What's the matter with you, hm? What is it now?"

Miss Besserman only shook her head. She kept her eyes on Mrs. Kay's shoes as long as they stood in front of her; and when they impatiently moved away again she sat blinking at the rug.

Mrs. Kay had gone back and begun throwing the bedclothes around. She stopped.

"Do you want me to take you to the bathroom?"

"No. . . ."

"I think you'd better—"

"*No.*"

Desperation made her quite loud—and stopped that purposeful approach. Mrs. Kay stood still a moment; then, with an exclamation under her breath, she changed direction and picked up the tray.

"I'll give you something lighter, this morning. Just

wait there, I'll be back. Or go on down to the bathroom, if you can make it. If you can't, I'll bring you a pan when I come back."

She went tight-lipped out the door, down the stairs. Back through the house. Her son was there, still in his dressing gown, pouring himself coffee at the stove. She passed him in silence and set the tray down sharply at the sink, beginning to flush the contents of cup and bowl down the drain. He watched her with cloudy wariness.

"Now what?"

"What difference does it make to you?" she snapped.

"Oh, come on—what is it? More trouble we don't need."

"No, we don't. Thanks to you."

He took fuddled offense, and went as far as the door with his cup. She moved around the kitchen as if he had gone, which began to worry him.

He blurted, "Christ—she's not dead, is she?"

"I asked you to get dressed."

"Look, don't ride me," he said, suddenly ugly. "I'll be dressed in time for anything that's liable to happen around here. Which is nothing! Out of this house is Howie's business, he gets paid for it."

"If Howie knew his business he wouldn't have brought her here. I don't want any more to do with Howie—I'm telling you that, and I mean it. This is the second one that's been too far along. They don't *get* to Howie until they're too far along. I don't want that kind. You tell Howie, no more."

"Oh, sure," he said. "Like, goodbye Howie, nice we knew you, don't come back. Like that."

She put a teabag in a small pot.

"Look," he said, "Howie is with us as long as he's *with* us. You know what I mean?"

"I'm sorry you ever got mixed up with him, he's got no sense."

"If he had sense he'd want too much," he replied, gathering confidence. "Besides, that's your lookout, isn't it? You can tell how far along they are before you start, can't you? So give back the money, tell her to get the hell out—Howie won't stop you! He'll do anything we say, and he'll keep his mouth shut whatever happens, so long as nobody tries to cut him loose. Howie's all right."

She poured boiling water in the pot, and over a dry nest of cereal flakes in a bowl. Relaxing, waking, he followed this procedure with puzzled eyes.

"What the hell are you *doing?*"

"I don't want her to have any more phenobarb for a while. Not till tonight."

"She's not sick, is she?"

"She'll be all right. She had extra last night, she hasn't used it up yet."

"Well," he said, doubtful.

"Get dressed, go on. I'm going to bring her down for a while, walk her around. You look in on Elva, you'll have to strip her bed and do a wash—I got to her too late this morning."

"Oh, *Christ.*"

She covered the tray and left it there, going out of the room. He followed, reluctant, in her wake.

"Why don't you take Elva? I can handle Violet. At least she's dry!"

She said nothing, walking ahead of him.

"This place is turning into an old ladies' home. Two of them! What for? All we need is one."

His mother stopped at the foot of the steps, raising a hand.

"Hush a minute . . . There, she's in the bathroom. She'll be all right."

His spirits rose with hers—as they would sink with them; and to cover this he said dourly: "Of course she'll be all right. She's tough as leather, those skinny ones always are."

"Well, Elva isn't." She went up, he following two steps behind. "Don't bump her around, now. All we need is something wrong with that one."

"Anything wrong with her isn't my fault. She's had it."

She gave him a look, at the head of the stairs, which he defiantly returned.

"Well, she has. You ought to put the other one back there, she's good for another ten years yet."

"Roddy, don't talk foolish. I'm too tired." She looked at him thoughtfully. "Get me Violet's teeth, I think I'll fix her some toast."

"I haven't had time to—"

"Just get me the teeth. Go on; here she comes. Say good morning to her."

She paused to watch the encounter; but it was so openly unsuccessful—Miss Besserman shrinking in silence from Roddy's obedient growl—that she thought it better not to seem a witness. Miss Besserman, tottering back into her room, found her hostess spreading up the bed.

"I think it might do you good to come downstairs

awhile this morning, Violet," she remarked. "Just let me have your dress, too, and I'll press it. You can wear your robe, no one will see you."

Absolute nothing. Not a word, not a movement.

Mrs. Kay turned and found Miss Besserman staring at her as if she were a shape in a dark room. Disbelief; incipient horror.

A bubble of rage broke silently in her mind. Under control, Mrs. Kay returned to her bedmaking to hide it. But her hands were hard on the quilts and sheets. What was the old scarecrow looking like that for? At *her*. A woman who'd shown her nothing but courtesy, first to last, and waited on her hand and foot into the bargain!

On top of all the rest, it was too much. Those insolent lawyers, not even bothering to reply to her summons . . . that insolent boy coming instead, where he had no business, and undoing all her patient work with the old creature . . . and now Howie, whom she couldn't offend, bringing that idiot girl to keep them up half the night and frighten the hearts out of them . . .

It was too much. She was going to let loose on somebody, pretty soon, if things kept on this way—and she wouldn't be the one to blame for whatever happened.

She could feel the violence of her own nature rising within her, rising up almost within taste, like some trickle of marvelous rare liquor . . . but a temptation she could not yield to, not yet.

But neither could she entirely suppress it. She allowed herself an abrupt departure from the room—only that. Abandoned the unfinished bed and went out, without another word. Shut the door behind her with ominous sharpness.

It would have given her satisfaction to lock it, too. But, after a pause, she put the key back in her pocket. Better not; there was the bathroom, in case she was going to be sick. And if she came downstairs eventually, so much the better—then some kind of apology would be in order for her ungratefulness.

Mrs. Kay went downstairs and threw away Miss Besserman's second breakfast. That gave her further small relief.

CHAPTER ELEVEN

THE GOOD WEATHER held, October pursuing its serene way in a series of bright and gentle days. The roses were loving it; and Tony made a mild foray into his mother's garden before he left.

She saw him struggling with his penknife among the bushes, and brought out the proper clippers to him. For which he was grateful.

"Who is getting all my Queen Elizabeth?" she asked mildly. "And I do mean all, don't I?"

"I'm just taking the nice ones."

"Yes, I noticed. Is this a new girl?"

"Not very," he said. "About eighty years new."

"You mean Mrs. Ryan? Again?"

She wasn't as pleased as she had been, and he looked over his arm to see why not.

"Yes," he said. "Why not?"

She didn't know why not; but her pleased interest was definitely evaporating. He put a final rose into the basket she was holding, and gave her his attention.

"Something about Dad? Mr. Bingham?"

Talking still went on behind his back—but not, apparently, in this case.

"No, no. I just wondered . . . if it's a good idea to get involved, after all these years."

He took the basket, and started her back toward the house.

"Well," he said, thinking about it, "the non-involvement wasn't deliberate, was it? I mean, wasn't it just that nobody happened to remember about her until this property deal came up? Or even then," he admitted. "I didn't go down there to see her, you know. Just the house. I only meant to say a civil howdy-do and ask to see around."

"Yes. Well, what happened to that?"

She wanted to do something to the roses, once inside, so he stood beside her while she began to wrap the stems in wet paper toweling.

"Let me cut off the thorns first," he suggested. "Big ones, aren't they?"

In turn, she waited upon him. He took out his knife again, trying to explain while he worked.

"Well, she was in an awful state about something— you remember I told you that. But I couldn't think what it was. Now it occurs to me that she probably doesn't understand what's going to happen to her at all. That dragon she lives with seems to have sold her the idea she's about to be thrown out on the street—probably so she'll fight to keep the house as it is. Which I think is what the dragon has in mind. Actually, Mr. Bingham says she'll have a nice new apartment in the building that's going up, and whatever help she needs in switching over. She might be rather glad to know it."

"But isn't it Mr. Bingham's place to explain all this? Surely he already has."

"Well, I thought I'd make sure the news got to her,"

he replied. "She's really up tight about something, that's for sure."

His mother packaged his roses for him in uneasy silence.

"What worries you about it?" he asked, patient.

"I don't really know. Except that if there *is* going to be unpleasantness about the house. . . ."

"There can't be, Mother. Apparently Mr. Bingham fixed it, way back there, so that Aunt Elva gets to occupy whatever is on the property, but not that specific house. He's very pleased with himself about it."

"I think he should be," she said loyally. Then he got a sudden smile, which surpised him.

"What?"

" 'Aunt Elva.' You haven't *got* an 'Aunt Elva'!"

"Well, I'm trying. . . ."

By the time he drove away she had left off smiling again; but at least, he felt, they had an amicable understanding.

The real problem was going to be the dragon.

He acknowledged this, and then put it to the back of his mind. The day was too fine, his pleasure in driving through it too real to spoil. Besides, this time he had taken the precaution of timing his arrival differently. By afternoon the old lady should be downstairs; and he was prepared to do some rapid and persuasive talking as soon as the door opened.

He had a more curious eye for his grandfather's old street this time, too. Leaving his car in the parking lot across from the house (the street was firmly posted against parking), he took time to consider the entire block. Except for some brave old maples, the prospect was rather dismal. He could see why no one had bothered, all these years. The houses were ancient without interest; the apartment houses—except for a newcomer next to the house—were surely from somewhere in the twenties. And the large expanse of parking lot that served the stores on the next street over didn't make for a very attractive view.

He knew a little more, now, about the couple who had come to live here after their marriage—as much as his father knew, which wasn't a great deal. Apparently Dr. Ryan had left one practice to take up another, here in new surroundings. But they couldn't have been elegant surroundings, even forty years ago. Had it been a street of professional offices then? Or was it his grandmother's money which had provided the staid house in Boston, still professionally occupied, where his grandfather's offices had been?

These were the things you didn't wonder about, until there was no one left to tell you. Except, possibly, Aunt Elva . . .

Glancing up, then, he saw her.

She was standing at an upstairs window watching him. When their glances met, her hand began to flutter at him—in agitation, not in greeting. He started to raise his own hand—the one that held her roses, to wave to her with her roses—before he realized that she was not waving to him. She was motioning to him to go away.

The patient yet feeble gesture was repeated, over and over. Go away, go away.

His arm fell to his side. He stood quiet, continuing to

look up at her, and her hand faltered and came down too. He could see her small face, very pale, with no expression that he could define except extreme seriousness. Then her lips moved; she began slowly shaking her head —turning it, rather, from side to side.

No. No. No.

His heart seemed to move in him—a queer feeling that startled him into action. He began to walk away on the same side of the street, in a kind of confusion that was new to him. It was as though he felt himself to be a danger to her, which she could not express nor he understand, yet which her weak message strongly conveyed.

He did not even look back until he reached the corner.

Then, very thoughtful, he leaned against a stop sign and looked down into the roses.

Either he was sliding from reality, or that was pure ESP.

Well, not all that pure. "Danger" he got, loud and clear; but to whom? If she was afraid for him, it would have given him great pleasure—expecially after that beating-heart bit—to go back and take on the jolly Kays.

But if to her, then what?

Did they give her a hard time, on account of him? Had they?

A middle-aged woman in slacks passed by, cheerfully saying: "Hi, flower-power! Got one for me?"

He transferred his thoughtful gaze to her backside, then pushed off into action. As he caught her up, she looked sideways at him, a little nervous, then stopped dead as he put Aunt Elva's roses in the top of her shopping bag.

84

"All for you. . . ."

She took a while, then called after him: "Hey . . . thanks! You're a good kid!"

He waggled a hand without turning, went on in longer and longer strides. Bailey, Mr. Bingham had said. No first name. He would have to call them all.

But there was only one attorney named Bailey, he found, standing over the directory in the nearest drugstore. And Bailey was in, and took his call without fuss.

Tony gave his name again. "From Boston," he explained. "Or, rather, Lincoln. I believe you're handling a local property sale for my father, on Brook Street?"

Mr. Bailey said he knew about the sale, and what could he do for Mr. Ryan?

"Well, I'm on your main street, here, and I wondered if you'd have time to see me if I came by."

No problem. Not yet, anyway. He got directions for finding Mr. Bailey, who was near enough so that Tony left his car where it was and walked. Over a bank, easy to find. New and prosperous offices. Trust Mr. Bingham.

Mr. Bailey let him in without much delay, and was as informally pleasant as his telephone manner. He didn't falter at it, even when Tony began by scrupulously disclaiming any mission from his father or Mr. Bingham.

"In fact, what I'm hoping for is some extra-curricular help," he saidl "You can take me on as a new client, if that would get you off any hook with Mr. Bingham."

"Is it about the house?"

"It's about who's in the house . . . Do you recall the set-up? The second Mrs. Ryan—my grandfather's second wife, that is—has a lifetime tenancy on the property. I

85

dropped by to take a look at my grandfather's place while it's still there, and met Mrs. Ryan for the first time. You understand she's no relation."

Mr. Bailey understood. He wasn't committing himself, but he was still pleasant.

"That was yesterday," Tony went on. "I got a strong impression that she was in some kind of trouble—specifically, in relation to the people who share the house with her. A Mrs. Kay and her son. He's thirtyish, and she's—well, his mother. Aunt Elva—that is, Mrs. Ryan seemed afraid even to talk to me. They never left her alone with me for a second. And the whole set-up seemed queer. Anyway, it bothered me enough so that I came back today—and she was waiting for me at the window of an upstairs room. Very upset, waving me to go away, shaking her head, all that. Very scared-looking. I didn't want to make trouble for her, so I went. Besides, I'm not at all sure they'd have let me in. I had a heck of a time getting in yesterday, and it didn't exactly turn into a friendship with the Kays. The old lady herself is very appealing, very gentle. And definitely scared.

"Well, the point of all this is," said Tony, to Mr. Bailey's continuing open look, "that I don't think she understands the position at all. Do you know if anyone's explained it to her?"

"You're speaking of Mrs. Ryan now," Mr. Bailey suggested.

"Mrs. Ryan, yes; but any of them. I think the Kays have convinced her that she's going to be thrown out into the street if the house is sold, and that they're trying to use her in some way to keep the place on for their own convenience."

86

"Won't do them any good," Mr. Bailey assured him.

"I know that—but does she? The Kays are pretty hard types, Mr. Bailey, and it's a tense situation over there. The only way I can see to end it is for someone official to get in to see Mrs. Ryan and explain to her how things really are. That she has nothing to worry about—she's got a new place coming up, and help in getting transferred to it, and so on. In other words, that she's not dependent on these people she's been living with, and that her rights are being looked after. You could do that, Mr. Bailey, if you would."

Mr. Bailey nodded, thoughtful now. He said: "Of course, you realize I haven't had any communication with Mrs. Ryan myself, up to now—that's been handled by Mr. Bingham's office. But I feel sure he's explained the situation to her. Didn't you ask him about it?"

"I don't think she sees her mail, past those two," Tony said bluntly. "And they've obviously interpreted Mr. Bingham's letter, or letters, as some kind of a proposal. Instead of a fact. He's very courteous about laying down the law, as you probably know."

Mr. Bailey said, with seeming admiration, that he did indeed. He added, "It sounds like a good thing for Mrs. Ryan that this sale has come up, doesn't it? When it goes through, there'll be no doubt about what's what, will there?"

"No," said Tony. "But meanwhile she's having a rough time."

Mr. Bailey moved in his chair.

He said, "You know, you have to consider other possibilities, Mr. Ryan. Such as the fact that her dependency on these people may be emotional, not rational. Her

87

whole attitude to them may be irrational—even senile. It's a fairly long-standing arrangement over there, I take it?"

"Yes. I know. I don't *think* she's senile," said Tony. "I think she's just a very scared old lady who doesn't know what's going on and has no one to tell her. But there's no way to be absolutely sure in advance, I suppose."

Mr. Bailey continued to regard him for a moment. Then, with another sharp movement in his chair, he said: "I'd have no objection at all to dropping by and seeing Mrs. Ryan, if Mr. Bingham has none. Suppose I get a letter off to him this afternoon. He may very well feel that this . . . visit should have been made before, circumstances being what they are over there. I'm sure Mr. Bingham assumed, as I did, that Mrs. Ryan was still in charge of her own affairs."

"How about a telephone call?" said Tony. "Do you want me to talk to him?"

Mr. Bailey smiled, very pleasant still, but not about to be rushed. He said he thought a letter would be preferable.

"We'll have it all clear and on record that way, and I should still be able to drop in and have talk with Mrs. Ryan within a day or so. After all, it's not as if she were in any, uh, emergency situation, is it? These are people she has lived with for many years—they probably understand each other better than you think, Mr. Ryan. But I do agree we had better make sure what Mrs. Ryan's condition is, if there's any question about it."

It probably didn't matter *why* Bailey went, so long as he went. And he had a nice good-guy manner, even if he

88

did think she was goofy he wouldn't show it.

You show *him,* Aunt Elva, he thought, walking back down Brook Street to get his car. Walking slowly, looking over at the now-vacant windows of his grandfather's house. He had no doubt, himself, as to her condition. She was scared. And felt herself to be helpless and alone in that fear. He still thought it was a rational fear.

Well, time would tell. Next day, or the next. He wished it could be sooner.

Hang on, Aunt Elva, he thought, standing a moment to see if she would come to the window again. The mounties are coming. . . .

She didn't appear. He found his car, and started back home.

CHAPTER TWELVE

Some women came to have their cards read, late that afternoon, and Roddy's rage threatened to become audible. He had never liked this activity of hers, perhaps because stupid children had teased him about it when he was smaller; and now he felt they had all the contacts they needed through himself and Howie. All the income, too.

She had to get him out of the house—send him over to the laundromat with Elva's sheets and gowns. For a few minutes she didn't think he was going to go.

"And what if Howie calls? It's just about the right time, we wait all day, and then you—"

"I'll handle it. Now go on, Roddy—I can't turn these women away, they're old customers and prominent women, too. We don't want any talk. Have you got change for the machines?"

"What's to *talk*? Just tell them you—"

"Roddy, get out of here. Go on. Get out or I will—and you can handle it yourself."

He needed firmness, always had, in his temper spells. And to real firmness he always yielded. However sullenly. To show him the reins were still in her hands, she added: "You'd better lock Violet in as you go by; here's the key. And put up the bars on Elva's bed, too—she might be restless. You didn't get her up today."

He muttered, and turned away. But it was all right. He would do as she told him.

She returned to the two well-dressed, cold-eyed women waiting in her glassed-in porch. Idly chatting, ready to do battle—for that was what it was. They came back time and again to challenge her, to prove there was nothing in it, to show that they were mistresses of their fate and she a charlatan. She charged them plenty, and made them feel something—as much as they were capable of feeling. A pang of doubt, a stirring of unease. Or of hidden excitement, if she was in a good mood.

She wasn't in a good mood today. In ominous silence, she laid out the cards, adjusted the lamp. Heard Roddy go out the door and down the porch steps. Heard something fall, on an upstairs floor.

Began, in a low, indifferent voice, to talk as if to herself.

". . . some trouble, some physical trouble . . . I see no pain, no pain yet, and yet I think something worries you . . . ? It should be attended to. . . ."

"*What* should be attended to?" Remote and icy. All nonsense.

Mrs. Kay looked across the table with blank, unblinking eyes—a stare that she could hold indefinitely. She allowed her voice to change, to become one of direct address.

"You know that I never give medical advice. Will you take up these cards, please? Put them to the right, face down. Thank you. Now please give me ten cards in two ranks. . . ."

Her voice fell back to its impersonal drone. The house was quiet around them, the day failing. The two women were still.

" . . . a young woman in your houshold, possibly a daughter? (This one had two sons.) Perhaps I should say, a young woman who comes to your house . . . frequently, I think?"

"She means the maid," said a flat voice.

"Yes, possibly . . . Small, fair? You have little direct contact with her? And yet she has a special awareness of you, I should say, an unfriendly awareness. There is possible conflict here. . . ."

They went away at last, as heavily doom-laden as she could make them, and she put their money into her cashbox with the money from last night.

Howie had not called.

Roddy stayed out rather longer than the washing and drying required—he had lost a dryer full of clothes, once, from not coming back in time to claim it. But it was possible that he had run into Howie at one of the bars nearby.

She went up to collect Violet's luncheon tray, overlooked, and see if she was ready for some supper. But the door was locked; Roddy had the key. She could have found another, up here, but she decided that a little more wondering might do Violet good. She was still acting up. So, giving the doorknob a hard rattle, she went off to the other end of the hall.

Elva was not acting up. She lay corpselike in her railed bed, in the nearly dark room, not even snoring. Mrs. Kay turned on the light, went over to her, and found that she had in fact become a corpse.

Her first reaction was one of extreme dismay. But by the time she had made certain that there was no mistake, that Elva was indeed gone, she realized how unnecessary this was. Pure habit had seized on her for a moment: the long habit of keeping Elva alive, in case she had to be produced. Of watching every dose, getting her up regularly, keeping her dry and fed and clean.

All done with now. Unnecessary, and done with.

Mrs. Kay left the room and shut the door behind her. Deep in thought, she went back downstairs. Not one to leave any situation unexamined, she was trying to decide if she had in fact overdosed Elva last night. Violet had certainly had a little too much; and she had been more careful with Violet's food than with Elva's. On the other hand, Elva had a pretty good tolerance by now . . . but she didn't move around or take nourishment the way Violet could. And neither Roddy nor she had paid much attention to Elva today. Had they even remembered her lunch?

She made a fresh pot of coffee, and was musing over it when Roddy came in. He was ready to be difficult—not a word; more bumping around than was necessary—but she no longer cared.

As soon as he reached the kitchen she said, "Roddy, are you sure Elva was alive when you cleaned her up this morning?"

He had just flung the bag of clean laundry down. Her inquiry froze him with one arm out.

"*What*—?"

"She's gone now," his mother said, impatient. "I'm

just wondering when it was. Try to think back."

"She's—you mean she's *dead*? Aunt *Elva*?"

He could still look like a small boy. But at the moment the sight didn't amuse his mother.

"Dead and pretty cool. I'm just wondering if you noticed anything when you put the railings up. Did you?"

"Jeez, I didn't—I didn't even touch her, I—"

"I didn't say you had, it's all right. Here," she said, pouring him a cup of the fresh coffee. "Wash some of that beer down, and don't be childish. Did you see Howie, by the way?"

"No—no—"

He sank down, took the cup. Fast but gingerly, he got the hot liquid down.

"I didn't— The railings were already up," he said finally. "I put them up this morning, when I changed her. . . . God, I don't know," he burst out. "You know how she was in the mornings, and I wasn't paying her much mind—"

"You mean you're not even sure about this morning."

"I *think* she was all right," he said helplessly.

The cup shook, he had to put it down. So abject, crouching there, that his mother could not resist a prod.

"You didn't snap her around, did you?"

"*No!* I *didn't!* Jeez, what a thing to—"

"All right. All right. I'm only teasing."

He stared at her, in some confusion of beer and shock, and she took pity on him—came and sat down at the table with him.

"As a matter of fact, it's a wonder she lasted this long," she told him. "She hasn't even known who we were for a

94

long time. And it wasn't all phenobarb, either. She didn't even know you—and you know how partial she was to you, Roddy."

"No," he said, numbly following. "That's right." Then, a last expletive: "*Jeez* . . ."

"I've been thinking what we'd better do," she went on. "It fits in pretty well, when you think about it. There's that place of Violet's—it's been on my mind, that we ought to get her to write a note to the super about being away for a while, just in case. But it's better this way. We'll have to take a look through her things, though, and see what she's got. I imagine it's mostly pension and social security, and whatever she got for that house she had with her sister. The sister had a daughter, somewhere down South—she would have got half, and I have a feeling Violet's just got her half in savings. The book ought to be there."

He said, "What do you mean, Violet? You said *Elva*—"

He wasn't following. Hardly even trying.

She kept on, patiently.

"We can pick up the book, we'll have to hold it awhile and see what we can think of. I doubt if the niece will come up here, or know much about Violet's affairs—she's got a family of her own. And we'll have to put that wig back, too. I can't decided what to do about the teeth. If we could only come across a spare, over there! But I suppose that's too much to hope for. I want her to eat well, though, she's peaked enough.

"Well, we'll look around tonight," she finished, under his frowning gaze. "When we take Elva over. I don't want Howie to have any part in this, though. I'm disappointed in him. Besides, it's none of his business—don't even mention it to him."

He continued to watch her, in numbed and frowning silence, as she got up again.

"I'd better fix some supper, now. And you take those sheets and things up. Unlock Violet's door and ask her how she feels—tell her I'll be up with her supper presently. She ought to be about over her sulks."

"Mom," he said, after an interval. Still from the table. "What?"

"I don't think we better do this. Try and pass Elva off for Violet. That's what you mean, isn't it?"

"Of course."

"I don't think we should do that. I don't think it'll work."

"Why not?"

"She doesn't— They don't look the same."

"Dead people don't look the same. Especially somebody that was all fixed up like Violet used to be. They'll allow for that. Besides, they won't find her right away, with any luck."

He sat on, sweating now, groping for more reasons. But reasons weren't his trouble, she knew.

"They might get in her own doctor. She must have one."

"I don't think so. Usually people just call the police. Besides, why should they think it isn't Violet? Who else would it be?"

"They still might get her own doctor. He might live there, or something."

"All right, what if they do? Even if they don't think it's Violet, there's nothing to say it's Elva. Is there?"

He looked at her in defeat. She got a little brisker with him.

"Now, come on, Roddy. I don't know why you're acting so squeamish about this. You're the one said we didn't need two of them, weren't you? Now it turns out we've only got the one. What else do you want to do?"

He didn't know. Opening and shutting his big hands, he sat frowning at them now.

"Go on up and let Violet out, now. You don't have to say anything if you don't want to. Then come down and we'll have supper, that's what you need, a little hot food."

"You want to take her over there tonight. Is that it?"

She didn't answer; they had talked enough for the time being. Accepting this, presently, he rose and took the laundry bag upstairs.

CHAPTER THIRTEEN

WHAT HAD SEEMED to Miss Besserman the longest, the most serious day of her entire life had come to a close. The signals of evening, already sadly familiar, came to rouse her from her unhappy drowsing: the strengthening shaft of light across the ceiling, from the streetlamp; the diminished sounds of traffic, as businesses and offices closed for the day. At last, the unlocking of her door.

It was Roddy who gave her her freedom tonight—her temporary freedom, of course, for she expected to be locked in again at bedtime. She knew his step by now too, and shrank in upon herself from the encounter.

But there was none. He only turned the key and withdrew it, stood there a minute, and then went back down the hall. She lay and listened until there was no more sound of him. Then—rather shakily, she was sorry to find—she got off the bed and went to peer out. The bathroom door was open, and she made that refuge without encounter.

She had brought her rose with her, and changed the water—tearing the stem a bit at the bottom. Refreshed, still lovely and serene, it leaned toward her in its jelly glass. What it had meant to her, during that day, he would never know. She did not even regret losing the others he had been bringing. And how fortunate that she had been looking out! To think of him coming into this place, not knowing what violence, what *wickedness,* it contained—perhaps running into real danger, because he did not understand what sort of people these were— had frightened Miss Besserman more than her own established troubles. Thank heaven he had understood her, and gone safely away.

For Miss Besserman knew well enough now what sort of place this was. You did not spend fifty years in the business world and remain ignorant of the darker side of life; no, you did not. Her own sister, who had been a married woman and borne a child, would have been horrified at some of the confidences Miss Besserman might have brought home with her . . . and did not. Especially had it seemed to her in these latter years that there was nothing, nothing at all, that people did not talk about—or do. She had tried to persuade herself that it was healthier this way; perhaps it was. Certainly it had been many years ago that she had given fifty dollars—a huge sum then—to a girl, to come to a place like this. A back-street abortionist. Because she had said, with utter and simple conviction, that she would take her own life if she could not raise that money. Miss Besserman had never digested the memory of this crisis—even though it had turned out rather flatly; the girl had gone away, and written once promising to return the money; that was all. But as the terrible secrecy of those times dissolved into unbelievable frankness, Miss Besserman had hoped that, at least, no young girls suffered so nowadays.

But it still went on. There were still people like the

Kays; still girls who came at night, and screamed in agony, and were bundled away—perhaps to die, from such clumsy surgery. And Miss Besserman was held to be a witness to it.

They had gone too far. She had, last night and today, passed some point where fear was relevant to behavior. Without knowing that such a state of mind was possible, she had entered into it. Her body still shook and grew cold with every alarm—and she paid no attention to it. They had pushed her too far.

She heard Roddy come out of his room and go downstairs. At once, she opened her own door. She was tired of the look of imprisonment—and what could it keep out? Besides, her clearing mind (and growing hunger; she had thrown away her lunch, after no breakfast) was beginning to plan.

She and her sister had grown up in an old house, and she knew that another key—almost any other key—would work this lock. Especially since they were foolish enough to take their key out each time they used it. Her first project was to go along the hall and find another key.

It was surprising how reluctant she was to leave this room, considering that it offered no real protection. And that a better refuge lay halfway down the hall, in the bathroom—she could always duck in there before anyone coming up could reach the top of the stairs. Still, she dawdled, passing nearer each time to her open door, yet passing it. Foolishly using up her energy, too.

At last she went out and stood near the top of the stairs. She could hear a far echo of kitchen sounds, an occasional vibration as of voices. They were not quiet people; and if this was all that reached her, of their activities, what could they possibly hear of her flitting around up here?

There were four rooms, besides the bathroom: hers at the front, Roddy's beyond that, and his mother's and Mrs. Ryan's at the back. She thought they would be less likely to notice their own doors than the old lady's, and so she boldly opened their doors, one after the other, and put in her hand to feel. No keys were there. It would have to be Elva's, then. She prayed that the poor creature would be asleep.

Her room was a well of gloom and silence; and Miss Besserman felt a rise of anger that they should leave her so. Very foolishly, she whispered: "Mrs. Ryan?" into the shadows. But no one stirred or answered.

Nor was there a key here.

She found one on her way back, inside a door she had taken for that of a linen closet but which gave onto the attic stairs. Two old dusty keys, in fact, lay on the ledge beside the steps. She took them both.

Both worked in her lock. In a tremble of possession, she found separate hiding places for them—and then continued to walk around her room, unable to settle. It was surprising how much energy returned to her with this small triumph.

Her tray arrived shortly after this. Mrs. Kay brought it, warily friendly. Miss Besserman turned her eyes at once from the large plate of macaroni and cheese, steaming and golden. There were strips of bacon with it, though. Surely these would be safe. And the rolls.

"We've had another try at fixing your plate, dear," said Mrs. Kay, producing it from her pocket. "See how it works. But be careful!"

What luck. Miss Besserman held out her hand, wordless, and closed her fingers over this treasure. There was a pause.

"You had better give me that dress," Mrs. Kay said finally. "I meant to press it today, but I think it's beyond that—it'll have to be cleaned. I'll give you one of Elva's tomorrow. She had some . . . has some nice ones she doesn't wear any more."

No. She must remain dressed. Looking down her front, Miss Besserman murmured: "I'll change after supper."

Mrs. Kay hesitated.

"Well, see that you do, Violet. I've had enough of this sleeping in your clothes."

Her temper was short tonight, but Miss Besserman saw that she did not want to lose it. She herself kept silent; and presently Mrs. Kay went out, an abrupt movement, and downstairs.

Scurrying to the bathroom, Miss Besserman cleaned her dentures as well as she could and restored them. How much else was restored to her, with them! And the rolls and bacon were hers now, in comfort and safety.

She went back and ate them, savoring every bite. So filled with purpose was she, by now, that the macaroni and cheese caused her no pangs of regret. She simply allowed it to congeal, by the window, and then put most of it into her paper napkin. The napkin she hid on the closet shelf.

Turning off her lamp, she lay upon the bed. This was the most anxious part. If she seemed to be already asleep, would they wake and undress her? The idea alone made it almost impossible to lie still. But the alternative was to lock herself into the bathroom—which might lead to unpleasantness. She could only hope that their obvious fatigue, and their carelessness too (for she had begun to find them quite haphazard, in many ways), would lead them to leave her alone until morning.

By morning she would be gone.

Someone came up onto the porch below: one person, a man, from the sound of it. The bell rang, and rang again; heavy steps shook the house, hastening to answer. Miss Besserman lay and listened. It was not young Mr. Ryan . . . or another unfortunate girl. Whoever it was was taken to the back of the house, in an insistent murmuring of male voices.

Some friend of Roddy's. A drowsiness came to her which she did not resist, since it came from no drug but from the luxury of being fed, of having two keys. And her dentures . . . She allowed herself naps, passing the time of waiting.

A slam of the front door woke her from one of these, and she heard the visitor running down the steps and then starting up a car, which drove away very fast. Would they remember her now? Would one of them come for her dress?

An interval of waiting stretched itself, in unbroken quiet. No one came. Her alerted senses dulled once more, and once more Miss Besserman dozed off.

CHAPTER FOURTEEN

AT SOME DARK and very still hour of the night she finished sleeping and woke completely.

No external agency had wakened her; none was necessary. She had always been able to set an internal alarm and obey it. Now she judged the time to be around two in the morning. Her watch, when she had quietly risen and turned on the lamp, showed her to be not far off: it was half after one.

The house, the street, were perfectly quiet. In equal quietness she tidied and brushed herself, and gathered up what she would take with her. Her bag; the stole, or shawl, that was part of her Elva-dress and would replace her vanished coat. The rose.

No. Reluctantly, she put it back, and examined her final appearance quietly. She saw the kind of elderly, shabby woman that she was accustomed to see, in this neighborhood, going on an errand in slippers and knitted shoulder-cover. White hair held back with combs, no makeup. She was glad of her dentures; they allowed of dignity to the expression, and a certain firmness. On the whole, she was not ashamed. The boy would have known her. She had a shy and almost friendly feeling that she knew herself.

She turned off the lamp. Now, if only they had taken

the key from the lock again . . . Slight anxiety sent her quickly to try. She found, after some confusion, that they had omitted even to lock the door.

What could it mean? That dreary, ready fear she was so tired of sprang up in her once more and made her fingers shake as she put away her prized and useless key. Anything unaccustomed now seemed trap-like to her, and she could not at once bring herself to go out into the hall.

Now that she noticed, her tray had not even been removed. But who had turned off the lamp this time? Had she done it herself?

Unable to remember, and in growing dismay, she began to walk softly from door to window, window to dresser to door, unable to commit herself. Then, putting down bag and shawl, she emerged as if on an innocent bathroom visit. Hall light burning. Closed doors. Darkness downstairs. She stood a moment, lost, then in timid resolve went back for her things and left her room for good, shutting the door behind her. An obvious runaway, if she were caught.

She reached the front door, and no one caught her. The door was secured by no more than a springlock, she had only to turn this with one hand and the doorknob with the other, and freedom opened before her.

She was outside.

Cold seized her, unexpected, making her pull the door shut behind her with clumsy haste, with noise. She stood appalled—then ran. A shuffling, clumsy run over the tippy porch and down the steps—the hard and solid pavement under her feet at last. She kept going, in a fast shuffling run that carried her into the shadow of the tree. There she stopped, but only for a moment. Her heart was a tumult in her, and she needed a long breath.

One last run, and she was at the apartment door. The vestibule was so brilliantly lighted! She had forgotten—or never noticed—that. She stood to one side to take out her key before she went in, but in the darkness could not find it in the change among which it was kept. There was nothing to do but push inside, stand under the light and look.

Under the light, she saw that her key was not there. She dropped change, spilled it into the depths of her bag, hunted among the paper money. Then, in total disorganization, she poured out the contents of her bag upon the floor and crouched to sort among that maddening jumble. It no longer mattered who saw her, what anyone might think.

All that mattered was that her key was gone.

It was gone. They had taken it. She knew this so finally, at last, that the knowledge seemed retroactive. She must have known all the while that they would take her key.

Still crouched like a pensive child, Miss Besserman restored her belonging to her bag. She already knew what she must do; and as soon as she had got herself upright again she pushed the superintendent's bell. Twice.

Time went by. Miss Besserman glanced blindly at the invisible dark outdoors. She felt no embarrassment about getting Mr. Sacher out of bed, no pity for him either—just the need to rouse him. Quickly. She rang twice more; and was raising her hand again when he answered on the house phone.

"What is it? Who is that?"

"It's Miss Besserman, Mr. Sacher—I've lost my key! Please let me in!"

"Miss Besserman . . ."

"Yes! Violet Besserman, in 3-D! I've lost—"

The release on the inner door began to buzz. She caught it, it yielded, and she was inside. Safe inside—almost home.

Warmth enfolded her, the outward and tangible evidence of her safety. Still shuddering a little, she went quickly down the hall and around the corner to Mr. Sacher's door. He wasn't there.

In weak irritation, she pressed the bell. How did he expect her to get into her apartment with no key? She had another wait before he peered out. Then he came out and looked down at her in astonishment.

"Miss Besserman—?"

"Yes—but I can't get in upstairs, Mr. Sacher! I have no key!" She almost added, *They took it*—and the effort to control herself made her voice break. He continued to stare down at her.

"Miss Besserman—something happened, you are all right?"

He was a wide, slow man who still had some trouble with the language and needed to get everything clear before he could proceed. She knew he did not mean to be rude, staring that way, but exasperation at his slowness almost made her cry.

"Yes—yes, thank you—but I want to go home! Please let me have my key, Mr. Sacher!"

"Yes, sure—sure. I get your key. You wait."

He vanished. Reappeared.

"You like to come in? Sit down, first?"

She looked at him in exhaustion. He rubbed his jaw and went away again. She could hear him fumbling at the key board and then he came back, keys in hand.

"Come on, Miss Besserman, I take you up now."

"You don't need to bother, Mr. Sacher—I'll bring you back the key."

"No, no. I take you. We go by the elevator here."

He held the door, watching her all the while in sleepy wonder. Helpless, she endured this.

"How are you out so late in the night, Miss Besserman? You are not ill?"

"No, I—I was coming home—"

He could not follow this; poor man, how should he? She added, remorseful: "I'm so sorry to wake you. I promise it will never happen again."

"That's all right, Miss Besserman. I know you are not like some. But I hope you are all right, eh?"

She looked down. They completed their ride in silence, and walked silently down her carpeted corridor— he understood by now that she did not wish assistance, or questions. But as he turned the key, pushed her door for her, he said—half reproachful to her secrecy:

"Now you stay home and be all right, yes?"

"Oh, yes—yes!"

In a surge of relief she stumbled past him, pressing the light switch, seeing at last what she had begun to fear she would never see again: her home, her own cozy living room, waiting as she had left it all those *endless* hours ago. All her things; her dear old things . . .

She gave a sudden cry, and stopped dead.

What was that heap lying by the bedroom door?

The *closed* bedroom door.

She never closed her bedroom door when she was alone.

One second of paralysis. Then she turned at once to leave. Mr. Sacher stood in her way, having pushed the door inward again at her cry. She clutched him, pushing.

"Mr. Sacher—please let's go, let me come down to your apartment awhile—"

He stood rocklike in her grasp, not answering, looking past her. She could neither pass him nor move him.

"Something frightens you," he said slowly, taking in the room. "What is it? What is this?"

He pushed past her and walked over to the heap, drawing upward some long piece of white material. Examined it, before turning to show her. In helpless fascination, she watched.

"But this is only a sheet from a bed," he explained, holding it up for her to see. "And this, this is a big bag, only. You see?"

A laundry bag. She saw; she understood nothing except that it was not hers, not her doing that it lay there.

"Mr. Sacher, please come," she whispered, half turned to run. "*Please*—"

But he was determined to dispel all her fears, and was turning the bedroom doorknob.

"I look all around for you, first, and then you are not afraid any more," he said, and walked into the lighted room beyond, and fell instantly, heavily, to the floor.

Muffled thumpings followed, and the fallen Mr. Sacher seemed suddenly to increase, to be more than one person, sprouting new arms and legs. Miss Besserman failed to scream—shrank against the wall, staring with disbelief, until the aperture widened and Mrs. Kay looked out of her own bedroom at her.

Then she ran.

Where, where?

Down the hall again, to where the elevator still waited. Pulling at the door, in a tangle of sliding stole and flapping handbag. Squeezing through, and turning at once to press hard upon the button marked 1.

The door closed, the elevator started its slow descent, and she fell back against the wall, scarcely conscious. She had abandoned Mr. Sacher . . . but what else could she do? All she could hope for was to escape, and to run for help quickly, quickly.

But where?

She knew no one in the building except to say good morning to—and none of these people would recognize her now. Oh, what did it matter—any door, any person! The elevator came to a stop. She pushed her way out and ran to lean on Mr. Sacher's bell, again and again.

Mrs. Sacher, come quickly. Come quickly.

The elevator stayed where it was.

The door to the firestairs opened, and Mrs. Kay came out, breathing hard. She stopped when she saw Miss Besserman so close to her. Neither of them said a word; but into the shock of silence between them a faint voice fell, from within the Sachers' apartment.

"Yes?" it said timidly. "Who is there, please?"

Mrs. Kay came up and put one arm around Miss Besserman's waist, and the other hand over her mouth. Her face was suffused with angry blood, her grip angry and hard. She half lifted, half dragged Miss Besserman around and pushed them both through the still-closing door to the fire stairs. Behind them the faint voice tried again: "Who is it, please? Who is there—?"

Miss Besserman did not even try to struggle. She only tried to remain conscious, and to obey the hard, hustling grip upon her, so that she should not be dragged senseless along the floor.

They went down, not up. A side door opened upon a narrow concrete walk which led to the street; and along this cold and silent way Miss Besserman felt herself being rapidly propelled, so roughly that the lost her footing more than once. It did not matter; Mrs. Kay sustained her, with the strength of fury.

They came out upon the sidewalk in the shadow of the wide maple which also touched the roof of the house. Their close-pressed rush along the public way was entirely private; a moment more and they were within the shelter of the porch.

Now Mrs. Kay spoke—directly into her ear.

"If you make one sound, I'll break your damn neck," she said.

Her hand then removed itself from Miss Besserman's mouth. Breathing hard, she found her key and used it— the musty house opened before them; and Miss Besserman was pushed inside.

CHAPTER FIFTEEN

M R. BINGHAM called me today about the Brook Street property," Tony's father said to him on the evening following his visit to Bailey. "What are you stirring up down there?"

"I don't know," said Tony. "Something, I hope."

"He wants to make sure we won't be embarrassed by having someone go to see your grandfather's widow. More or less on our behalf."

"It's sort of late to start wondering about that, isn't it? I've already been."

"So your mother tells me. With roses."

"Did you tell him it was okay?"

"What, the roses?"

"About Bailey," said Tony, not amused.

"Who's Bailey?"

"Oh, come on, Dad!"

"You mean the local man? Our representative once-removed? Bingham didn't even mention his name—that's how remote we're keeping it." He grinned at his son, who smiled back in relief. "I understand you're indignant about the way we've neglected this lady."

Tony shook his head.

"Mr. Bingham never said that."

"No, he didn't. But when you start hounding the lawyers about her, all of a sudden, and going down there yourself with all your mother's best roses, what do you expect us to think? You didn't have to keep it such a private enterprise, Tony. She isn't forbidden territory. Certainly not now that your grandmother's gone."

"Was she before?" Tony asked.

"Not really; no. I think mainly we just forgot about her. There wasn't any inducement to remember. It had been a painful time for your grandmother, naturally."

"She doesn't seem like a home-wrecker," said Tony thoughtfully.

"Very few eighty-year-old ladies do," his father replied. "Besides, I'm not sure that she was. In any case," he added, dropping the subject as the Ryans always did, "I told Mr. Bingham I thought it was a very good idea for his man to go and call on her and help her get straightened out. There's nothing she can do about the sale, and we might at least be as helpful as we can. I'm glad you thought of it."

But Tony said perversely, "I wish I'd thought of her a long time ago. I don't think she's been having much of a life in that house, with those people she shares with."

"Well, it's been a depressed area for years," said his father, as if this explained everything. "I'm afraid they may still run into trouble, developing it. Mr. Bingham tells me the superintendent of the apartment house next door to our property was murdered last night. It was in the papers today. That isn't the kind of thing that encourages upgrading."

"He was *murdered*?"

"Apparently. Haven't seen it myself."

"But that's fantastic, Dad! It isn't *that* kind of a district. . . ."

He couldn't explain his dismay, even to himself. All that came into his mind was the memory, the very still memory, of his grandfather's house. The old rooms, the empty office with its diplomas—and upstairs, at the window, an old lady warning him away . . .

He got up, a restless movement.

"Well, that's a cheerful piece of news," he said helplessly.

His father seemed surprised by his uneasiness.

"It is shocking, of course. All this spreading violence is hard to understand. It shouldn't have any effect on the sale, though—that's pretty well settled. Or on your new protégée, for that matter. What sort of building is it, next door?" he asked, as his son continued to frown.

"Oh—new. One of those brick-and-glass places with balconies. Biggish."

"Well, there you are," said his father. "Comparative affluence in a depressed neighborhood—I suppose the poor fellow caught some sneak-thief going through."

But it was stranger than that, Tony found, when the next morning's paper carried a more complete story. The superintendent—one Albert Sacher, 56—had been found dead in the third-floor apartment of one of the tenants, a Miss Violet Besserman. Miss Besserman, described only as an elderly woman who lived alone, was also found dead on the premises—but apparently of natural causes. Sacher's death had been violent: from a blow on the head, followed by strangulation. Mrs. Sacher said that someone had rung their bell at around

114

two in the morning, and her husband had left his bed to answer and never come back. She had later answered another ring at their bell and found no one there. When her husband did not return she called the police; and by tracing the missing key, the bodies were discovered. No one had seen or heard anything unusual.

It made a curious story, and its effect on Tony was haunting. Perhaps because of the elderly woman who lived alone in her apartment, as Aunt Elva would, and had been invaded anyway. But she hadn't died of that invasion, unless there was some mistake. Or of any other violence. Then what was the connection with the superintendent's death, and what was he doing there at two in the morning?

Curious; and haunting. The more so because of his own uneasy experience, almost on the spot, only a few hours before.

He went so far, later in the day, as to try and telephone the old lady—just to say hello, and to tell her that a friendly sort of lawyer was coming by to offer whatever help he could. But she had no telephone listed. He asked if one were listed to the name Kay, on Brook Street, and was given a number. But he was put off by its not being Aunt Elva's telephone; and he did not make the call. Instead he called Bailey, who was as pleasant and alert as at their meeting. He said that, with Mr. Bingham's approval, he was now about to contact Mrs. Ryan and would be in touch with Tony as soon as he had anything to report.

The following morning Tony had the honor of a letter from Mr. Bingham, which his mother presented to him without any comment. She did not even hover while he read it. But he ran into her very soon afterwards.

"You seem to have made quite an impression on Mr. Bingham, dear," she said wistfully.

"Oh—sorry," he said. "Take a look at it—it's on my desk." Then he escaped downstairs. She was going to be as puzzled as he; and he hadn't yet decided what his position should be.

Mr. Bingham had written:

My dear Tony,

Regarding the sale of your grandfather's property, and the resettlement of the second Mrs. Ryan: Mr. Bailey has twice attempted to make an appointment to see this lady. So far he has been unsuccessful. He tells me that he was first told by her companion (in whose name the telephone is listed, by the way) that Mrs. Ryan was ill, and then that she did not wish to receive an attorney's visit at all in her present state of health, but would be willing to see you at some future time. I suggest that there is no real object to be served in pursuing the matter at this point, and that we allow Mr. Bailey to call on her at a later time when matters are more advanced and when the lady's health will, hopefully, have improved.

It was a great pleasure to see you the other day, and I hope you will come down and have lunch with me one day soon. My best regards to your parents.

What was he to make of this? Was the invitation really from Aunt Elva, who had so urgently waved and nodded him away from the house? Or from Mrs. Kay who had danced with impatience to get rid of him last time?

Or was Aunt Elva's sudden illness real? Like, in the head?

He didn't believe this. He didn't believe much in the illness bit anyway. But what was the point? He thought Aunt Elva far too gentle and timid to have delivered the ultimatum Mr. Bailey had got; but was puzzled that Mrs. Kay should fabricate it. Was he, Tony, supposed to be the lesser of two evils? But there was no pressure on them to see anyone. Why did they want him to come?

His mother came downstairs after him presently, with her familiar look of disguised intention.

She began by saying, "I brought the letter down, in case you want your father to see it."

He said that was fine.

"You seem to have made quite an impression on Mrs. Ryan, too."

"I think it was your roses," he said.

"Yes, well, the thought was yours. But I don't really see," she said, smiling, "that all the responsibility is. Do you?"

"I don't know. I'm not sure I know what the responsibility is, let alone whose."

She seemed a little relieved.

"Well, let's see what your father says. It can't be anything urgent, after all these years, can it?"

"I don't know," he said again.

But why did he feel urgency growing out of this much-filtered message, so obscure to begin with? Half exasperated, he decided to accept Aunt Elva's invitation (if it was one) and try to clear up the muddle in one last visit. If that failed, over to Bingham and Bailey. After all, when moving day came on Brook Street, the thing would settle itself. He had only hoped to reassure the old lady beforehand—and maybe that was still possible.

So on Sunday morning (he had juggled his time as much as he dared on weekdays, for a lowly sophomore) he called the Brook Street number. He got the son. Or some male who said "Yes?" and then waited. Tony opened with a mild prod.

"Is this Mrs. Ryan's house?"

Pause. Then: "Who is this?"

"This is Tony Ryan. Could I speak to Mrs. Ryan, please."

Could he? Son thought.

"Just a minute."

The silence of the house flowed along the wires to him for a while. He neither expected nor got Aunt Elva. But the second voice was unexpectedly placating.

"This is Mrs. Kay speaking," it said, and might have been forcing itself through a tight smile. "Mr. Ryan?"

"Yes . . . Is Mrs. Ryan there?"

"Oh, yes. I'm sorry she doesn't feel up to coming to the telephone. She's very upset about this business of her house, you know—some lawyer keeps trying to talk to her about it, and it's upset her a lot. I wonder if you know anything about that."

"Well, this is just a personal call," said Tony. "I thought I might drop by and see her for a few minutes this afternoon."

"Is this about trying to sell her house, Mr. Ryan?"

"No, that's not my business," he said, patient. "Will you tell her I'll be by about three, just to say hello?"

"Well, it would be a help to her if you could set her mind at rest about that lawyer, you know. She's never going to agree, but it upsets her to have to keep saying so. She's a good-natured woman, Mr. Ryan, but, after all, this is her home, she doesn't have all that many years left to enjoy it, and it doesn't seem right to keep bothering her this way. I hoped you could do something about that."

"I won't bother her," he said. "About three o'clock, then?"

"I don't know that you ought to come at all unless you can bring her some good news, Mr. Ryan," she said bluntly. "She'll be expecting some kind of news from you, after all—and if it isn't good it's bad, that's only reasonable."

"All right, let's say it's good news, then," he said deliberately. "Tell her that. And I'll come around three."

"Well, I hope you mean what you say," she said obstinately. "You're old enough to realize what a disappointment can mean to an elderly person, Mr. Ryan, and she's been counting on you to help her with these lawyers. Don't disappoint her, now."

He hung up angry—a tribute to the woman's force and persistence, for he had thought himself on top of their ridiculous exchange right up to the end. But he wasn't on top of anything—nor even sure he was right in going down there again. What kind of a business had he got himself into? Maybe Aunt Elva liked having this female bulldozer on her side—maybe she had been waving him away for Mrs. Kay's sake, not her own. Maybe this was good old symbiosis, in working model, and he was telling himself stories about sweet little old ladies.

For ten cents he wouldn't have gone.

To make it worse, his mother cut some of her roses for him. He went out to his car clutching them glumly, forgetting about thorns, and bled and sucked blood all the beginning of his journey.

CHAPTER SIXTEEN

THEY WERE NEARER November, now, and the weather had broken. Golden days were intermittent, growing rarer, and there had been two days of rain that beat the wild garden down for its winter kill. Still, a lot of thicket and stalk would remain, Miss Besserman thought, sitting by the garden view that was now hers. It was a piece of ground that would have character under snow, almost like countryside.

She had not seen the garden in winter from either this window or the window of her lost apartment—such a short time had she lived in this neighborhood. She quietly faced the possibility that she would never see it in winter. The Kays, to whom her fortunes now seemed to be fastened beyond hope of detachment, had somehow managed things badly. God knew what would become of them all. Or what had become of Elva Ryan. They said she was in a nursing home for the time being, and that Violet might as well enjoy the view and the sun, when there was any, until she came back. But she was not coming back. Miss Besserman understood that.

Whether she had died of her years or of some mishandling, they had lost her; and Miss Besserman would be kept as her replacement as long as they needed one. But she did not think they would succeed in this plan either.

Whatever crisis they had already bungled—something to do with Elva, or that poor girl in the night, or the savage attack on Mr. Sacher—whatever it was, it had shaken Roddy severely. He no longer left the house at all, that Miss Besserman could hear. No doubt he feared that Mr. Sacher had glimpsed him and would recognize him . . . or else it was something to do with the girl, or with the man who came and quarreled. There was no way of knowing. But of one thing Miss Besserman felt certain: they had bungled things beyond repair in this place. Before too long, Mrs. Kay would have to acknowledge this and give up her fight—lose whatever unspeakable professional connections she had and valued, and go somewhere else with Roddy. They would have to begin again, ruthless and incompetent, in some new place—or else Roddy would go to pieces. Mrs. Kay was deceiving herself if she thought otherwise. Miss Besserman, with nothing to hope for either way, found it impossible to deceive herself. She was nearly at the end of her last usefulness.

The night of her escape and recapture had been a turning point for her too. The shock of that experience had nearly finished her; and for several days—she did not know how many—she hardly knew where she was or what had happened. Possibly Mrs. Kay had, as she liked to insist, "brought her round." Miss Besserman did not think so. The end of her life might be at Mrs. Kay's disposing, but not its continuance. However, this belief in one success, amid so much disaster, had softened her hostess's feelings toward her in a curious way, which Miss Besserman noticed without any emotion. Mrs. Kay had come to treat her almost as if she really were Elva, restored to her senses.

Or perhaps it was simply that, with Roddy removed from her in nervous gloom, she had no one else.

Whatever the reason, the key turned in Miss Besserman's lock far oftener than necessary these days, and Mrs. Kay would come in, sometimes persuasive, sometimes grumpy, sometimes fuming from some other encounter, and brush around the edges of Miss Besserman's impassivity for a while. Fortunately, between convalescence and whatever drugs she was being given, Miss Besserman did not care.

When she heard hard footsteps now, and the turning key, she did not even look around from the garden. She continued to watch a neighborhood cat stalking the grackles, who were well aware of it.

"Well, Violet," said Mrs. Kay's voice. The tone of it established her mood: persuasive. Miss Besserman was not surprised when Mrs. Kay came around and sat partially in her view, on the edge of the bed.

"A little sun today, hum?" she said, following Miss Besserman's gaze with a brief glance. "Well, we won't get much more of that for a while. But this is the warmest part of the house, back here. You're warm, aren't you?"

"Yes," said Miss Besserman.

"Your eyes look better, they've lost that ghastly look they had. You were a sick girl, you know. I had quite a time with you."

"Yes . . ."

Mrs. Kay leaned over and adjusted the set of Miss Besserman's collar.

"That's simply too big for you. Elva wasn't really a small woman. for all she lost so much flesh these past years. Her bones were bigger."

A small shudder took hold of Miss Besserman, meaningless. She continued to watch the garden. (But it was typical of Mrs. Kay that she never bothered to refer to Elva inthe present tense.)

"Chilly?"

"No . . ."

"If you'd only behaved yourself, you'd have your own things to wear. All the trouble we took, to go over and get them for you, and then you had to spoil it."

In the pause that followed, Miss Besserman was aware of being watched. To see if she believed this. What difference did it make? It was not her things that were lost, it was she; and whatever alarm Mr. Sacher had raised, no one had thought to come and look for her here. No one ever would.

At about this point in their lifeless dialogues Mrs. Kay would begin to show irritation.

"Goodness knows what'll become of them now," she said cruelly. "And they were nice things, too. That fur coat was still very handsome, Violet—you had years of good use left in that."

An idea of her Persian lamb coat, such an achievement, so prized, rose up slowly in Miss Besserman's mind. She turned and stared at Mrs. Kay, uncertain.

"What did you do with my coat . . . ?"

(Foolish; foolish. She saw the satisfaction in that watching face and turned her eyes back to the garden.

124

But too late . . .)

"What did *I* do with it! Now that's a silly question, isn't it? If I'd had a chance to do anything with it, it would be safe here with you, along with all your other nice things! But you couldn't wait for that, could you? You had to make a fool of yourself running around half-dressed in the middle of the night, waking everybody up and catching your death of cold . . ."

But the satisfaction was dying out of Mrs. Kay's voice. The evoking of that night was no pleasure to her either. She got up from the bed and walked around somewhere behind Miss Besserman, her discontent presently breaking out.

"The idea of bringing that man up there! What could you expect—bursting in like that? Roddy's no coward, nobody can say he is—he'll stand up to any man, if he has to. But he's high-strung, too, he always was, and anybody that knows him knows better than to take him by surprise like that. . . ."

She stopped—stopped talking and moving, somewhere in the background. In the sunlit silence a sparrow lit on the windowsill where Miss Besserman could see every detail of his little coat, its pattern hidden to a distant eye. She watched it with comfort, some sense of loss subsiding in her, until movement within the room made him flit away.

Mrs. Kay, without any more talking, went out and shut the door behind her. She didn't bother to lock it; often she didn't. It made no difference to Miss Besserman.

But some obscure sense of release made her lean forward a little, extending her line of vision so that she could see the apartment house next door. The puzzle was that she could never be sure from here which were her windows. There were so many of them, with their venetian blinds and glass curtains, and almost no signs of occupancy, nothing to orient her. She would at last, in easy fatigue, pick a window that might be hers and lean and stare at it, trying to put her thoughts beyond the obscuring curtains to the waiting and familiar room beyond. Either room, it didn't matter. Perhaps it was her bedroom, with its firm bed tidily made up, the blue-flowered sheets smooth under her mother's crocheted spread, all the family photographs and snapshots on the dresser, on the walls. . . . Or the living room with the settee newly upholstered in blue velvet, such a lovely piece that her niece would be glad of someday, well-kept and polished, not a scratch on it.

Nothing could happen to her things, could it? Mr. Sacher would know this was not her fault, that she would come back if she could. When the rent came due and she was not there to pay it, surely they would wait until she could? She had always been so prompt in paying her bills, her credit was very good, surely they would understand and wait and not disturb her house?

Was it the first of the month yet? Past the first? In a confusion of haste Miss Besserman struggled out of her chair and went to look for her bag, which was somewhere here, she had seen it not long ago. Her checkbook was there, she could write a check for her rent and they could mail it for her—surely they would do that.

The bag was found and its contents tipped out on the

dresser; she did not have the energy these days for polite digging. The little checkbook was there, folded so neatly upon itself, and she seized it with gratitude and went out into the hall and down the stairs. The journey seemed very long; she shuffled along in her felt slippers, old friends by now, and held on to whatever came to hand in passing.

They were in the back of the house, in the garden room, sitting across the table from each other. Mrs. Kay had her cards spread out between them; but whether she was reading Roddy's fortune or her own, it was a listless performance, and quiet. Roddy was drinking something and staring down, his mother slowly manipulating her cards. Neither of them seemed startled by Miss Besserman's appearance. Roddy, whom she feared, only glanced at her and away, frowning.

She said timidly to Mrs. Kay: "I must pay my rent."

Mrs. Kay looked up without interest. then, glancing at her son, she made an effort.

"What have you got there, Violet? Let me see."

"It's my checkbook. I had better make out a check for my rent. You will mail it for me, won't you?"

"Let me see," Mrs. Kay repeated, holding out her hand. Helplessly, Miss Besserman put the checkbook into it, and Mrs. Kay unsnapped and opened it, riffling through the stubs. She remarked, as if with regret, "You had a nice balance. Almost four hundred."

"Yes, there's plenty to pay my rent, and . . ."

Miss Besserman stopped with a sudden low cry, which made them both look at her again.

"My checks—what happens to my checks? My mail—

my checks should go to the bank—"

Roddy wasn't liking her noise, and his mother's voice sharpened to put an end to it.

"You're mail is perfectly all right, Violet! They'll hold it for you, don't make such a fuss. Now write your check, and run along upstairs—have you got a pen?"

She got up and found one, as the telephone out in the hall began to ring. Roddy looked up; but his mother said: "I'll get it."

Without argument, he simply rose and left the room ahead of her. She put the pen down at random and followed him. Miss Besserman, after a moment of uncertainty, got hold of the pen and sat down to make out her check while she could.

It was an unexpectedly difficult chore. Her fingers seemed not so manageable as they had been. Her first effort was so unfamiliar-looking that she destroyed it and began again—was just signing her name, much more recognizably this time, when Mrs. Kay returned alone.

"Well, Violet, you'd better go up and get tidy," she said. She seemed livelier. "You're going to have a visitor this afternoon."

Absorbed, Miss Besserman finished writing, and detached the check.

"Here it is, Mrs. Kay. You will mail it?"

"Of course. Did you hear what I said? That young man you like so much is coming to see you—Mr. Ryan. And I think he'll have some good news for us this time. How about that?"

"Yes . . . Do you know where to send it? I could address an envelope."

"All right. But not now. You remember him, don't you? The one that brought you the rose?"

"Yes."

But a confusion began in her, as she sat there with her eyes on the precious check so carelessly held.

"He's coming *here?*"

"He certainly is—and pretty soon, too. Now go up and start tidying, and I'll bring you some lunch. Get up, Violet!"

Miss Besserman got up. Knowing it was somehow the wrong thing to say, she still persisted: "I had better address an envelope for you."

"Later," said Mrs. Kay, less cordial. "Now run along, I want to straighten this place up. Are you all right, or do you want Roddy to help you?"

It was a small threat; and Miss Besserman responded by setting herself in motion. She kept tight hold of the pen, though; and Mrs. Kay, if she noticed, said nothing about that.

CHAPTER SEVENTEEN

SHE WASN'T PLEASED to see him at all.

His reception was topsy-turvy this time: the dragon all modified cordiality, Aunt Elva as steadily watchful as a little figurine. Last time he had hardly been able to get her to look at him. This time—gravely, fixedly—she kept her eyes on him and yet, when he met her look, there was no response. She wasn't seeing him at all, he thought. She was only watching.

They had her downstairs and ready for him when he arrived—sitting in the chair where he had left her last time. The dragon brought him in and showed him where to sit. Not too near. Then she sat down too. No sign of Little Boy Bluebeard.

He had stopped to lean over the old lady and give her the now-dethorned roses. She was so intently watching him that he had at last to lay them in her lap to call them to her attention. Only her hands acknowledged the gift, spreading over the roses like a light, protective net. But she didn't look at them.

It was Mrs. Kay who said, "Well. Aren't they pretty. Elva?"

"Yes," she said then. "Yes . . . thank you."

But she couldn't take a minute off to look down and see.

Interested, disappointed, he went and sat down. Otherwise she was going to get a crick in her neck.

"Well, you're looking very pretty, Aunt Elva," he began—although "pretty" wasn't the word for that pale, intent small face. Not even "appealing." No appeal was there any more. Only a kind of desperate, contained aliveness. He began to wonder if she really had been ill.

"I'm glad you're better," he went on. "Did you have a bad time?"

"Yes," she said, as if surprised that he should know this. "Oh, yes . . ."

"She's been a very sick girl," Mrs. Kay confirmed. "This is really her first day down. I thought it would do her good to hear some good news."

He looked at the old lady with increasing thoughtfulness. Just for the moment, he found himself as disconcerted as his parents by this new involvement. What had seemed simple in plan—to make sure she knew of the advantages and help available for her—now struck him as almost irrelevant. He had an uneasy sense of a complicated tangle of lives here that he didn't know enough about to interfere with.

But he had to try, now that he was here.

"Well, I don't know," he said—an opening phrase of his father's, which he was startled to hear himself using. "What I wanted to talk over is more along the lines of a pleasant idea—at least, I hope you'll think so. Do you remember Mr. Bingham's letter, Aunt Elva? About the sale?"

"There isn't any sale, Mr. Ryan. You know as well as I do that there can't be, during Mrs. Ryan's lifetime."

He was too intently feeling his way to be irritated by the interruption.

"Well, I'm afraid that isn't true," he said carefully. "What Mrs. Ryan has is a lifetime occupancy of whatever building is on the property here—but there's nothing to say what the building must be. Which just means," he went on, to his grandfather's widow, "that you'll have a new apartment, in the building they'll put up here, for as long as you want it. And all the help you need in getting resettled, and moving. Did you understand that, from Mr. Bingham's letter?"

Mrs. Kay suddenly got up.

"You're wasting your time, Mr. Ryan. And ours. I'm sorry I let you come." With sudden fury, she said: "Mrs. Ryan will never agree to leave this house! How many times do you have to be told that? She is never going to agree!"

"Mrs. Kay, she doesn't *have* to agree," he said, restrained. "Will you please stop interrupting, and let me explain this to her?"

"No I will not," she said rapidly. "You got in here under false pretenses, and we don't want to hear another word from you! And I'll tell you something else—you haven't got the only lawyers in the world, you know. If you want to make a nasty public scandal about trying to put this old lady out of her legal home, then you just go ahead and try! You'll find we can get lawyers just the same as you can!"

"I doubt it," he said, getting up too. "There is no case to argue—and if you can't understand that, perhaps you had better go and talk to a lawyer about it. If you can explain to him just what business it is of yours," he added, with a rise of anger. He swallowed that, remembering the silent old lady below them.

Mrs. Kay pounced on the pause.

"I certainly can! She hasn't got anybody in this world that's shown the slightest interest in her but us—till you and your lawyers come along and want to put her out of her house! Fifteen years of the best care and consideration—"

"Mrs. Kay, that's enough," he broke in, low and fast. "I didn't come here to argue with you, I came here to talk to Mrs. Ryan—and I'm going to talk to her, if I have to get a court order to do it and come back here with a policeman. Now is that the way you want it?"

"She has nothing to say to you," she said, taken aback.

"Then let her say it."

He sat down again, pulling his chair nearer. He could hear Mrs. Kay breathing heavily, standing behind him, but at least she was quiet. He took a deep breath of his own, and sent a worried look at Aunt Elva.

He needn't have worried. She sat there like a bird, still and watching. A bird on the other side of the windowpane.

"I'm sorry," he said anyway. "And I'm sorry about your house, if you really mind leaving it. This whole thing was drawn up years and years ago, and there's nothing to be done about it—but I hope you'll like the idea of the new apartment. It ought to be nice—rather like the building next door, with balconies and so on. Will you like that?"

She suddenly looked down, for the first time. He

could *feel* Mrs. Kay standing behind him, in fierce self restraint; but nobody answered him at all.

"*Do* you mind leaving the house, Aunt Elva?" he persisted.

She was going to answer, this time. He felt sure of it from the way her eyes moved—upward and past him, then back.

She said, in a small voice: "Now?"

There was a kind of snort from behind him.

He answered as well as he could.

"Well—I don't think you're up to a ride just yet, do you? When you are, I'd love to take you for one. Maybe to find someplace very pleasant for you to stay, while they're building the new apartment. Would you like that?"

"Now I think you've just about had your say," a hard voice remarked, above him. "She isn't well enough yet to listen to any more of this nonsense—and I'll ask you to leave right now, if you've any consideration left. You've said what you came to say, and I hope you're real proud of yourself."

He heard her out, and made no answer. This was still all the home and care the old lady had, until he could get things moving to get her out of here—which he meant to do, as soon as he got back to Boston. Meanwhile, when he left, she would stay. No use making it worse for her than it obviously was.

If he had been his father—or in his father's position of authority—he would have got her out of here instanter. That very day. Damned if he wouldn't. But he had no authority, and very little power, and he was much aware of the lack just then.

"Well, think about the new place," he said, reaching out and taking one of her hands. It clung to his. "Everything will be pretty and new, and they'll fix it up for you however you like. You can sit out on your balcony when it's nice, and look over the world."

"Elva, you'd better come upstairs and rest, you've had enough silliness for one day."

Mrs. Kay pressed between them, roughly separating their hands, presenting him with her back. He got up as civilly as he could, moving to where he could see Aunt Elva. She was looking for him.

"Goodbye for now," he said. "Think about better days ahead. I'll be back as soon as I can."

"Save yourself the trouble—unless you want to come with a court order," Mrs. Kay said. Daring him. "You're turning her out for your own benefit—don't pretend any different. And don't come back here."

He went toward the hall without answering. A small cry behind him made him stop, and turn.

"*Your name . . .*" the old lady was crying after him, in some escape of confusion.

His heart sank a little, and Mrs. Kay made a vexed sound.

"You've got her all turned around, her mind's as clear as mine when you don't come here and devil her," she said angrily. "And don't you say it's not!"

He ignored her.

"I'm Tony, Aunt Elva. Tony Ryan. And we're still out in Lincoln, in case you want to reach us. I'll be back as soon as I can."

"Get *out,*" said Mrs. Kay, in a lash of fury.

He walked out and shut the door behind him with restraint—as angry and sick at heart as he could ever remember being in his entire nineteen years.

CHAPTER EIGHTEEN

R ODDY, where did you put those letters we got from Elva's lawyer?" his mother demanded, coming into his room.

He was lying on his bed reading a paperback; and he slammed this down with the fast temper that was getting on her nerves so badly these days.

"God, can't you knock?"

"Now don't give me any moods, I've had enough between Elva and that rotten Ryan kid—while you were up here in peace. Where are they?"

But he only stared at her, queerly furtive.

"Not Elva. Violet."

"I mean Violet."

He gave her another sideways glance and sat up, bracing his arms on the bed's edge.

"He's gone, then?"

"Gone and not coming back, whatever he thinks," she replied briefly.

"I told you it wasn't going to be that easy. What did he say?"

"Nothing that matters, or that I'd bother repeating. Where are the letters?"

"How should I know?" he said, flaring again. "You kept them."

"I gave them to you to show to that friend of Howie's. Don't you even remember?"

He sat looking at her, uneasily defiant. She controlled her impatience.

"Well?"

"Well, of course I remember. His brother-in-law's a lawyer. I thought it might be a good idea for him to look them over. I can get them back."

He started to get up, with a new look of interest, but she put a hand on his shoulder.

"Never mind. I told you, I don't want you calling Howie any more. That means about anything."

"Then how am I going to get the letters back? I'll just ask him for the letters, that's all."

"No." She went over and sat down in his easy chair—a weary slump. But her eyes remained steady on his. "We're finished with Howie. Can't you get that through your head? How much proof do you have to have, that he's nothing but trouble?"

He muttered, "I don't know why you keep on blaming him about that girl. It was her fault she let it go so long—and she lied to him. How was he supposed to know?"

"I'm not talking about that, I'm talking about after. Dumping her in a motel that way! She had people, they would have had some reason to keep their mouths shut —but he didn't have the guts to go near them, did he? So now it's a police case, thanks to him—and don't think he's out of the woods yet. People turn up after weeks, sometimes, that saw something and didn't know if they should mention it or not. And I suppose he borrowed

138

that car from some other no-good."

"No, he didn't! He just—"

"Never mind. It's still a mess, and I don't want you to have anything to do with him again. About *anything*. In fact," she said, watching him steadily, "I'm thinking very seriously about our getting out of here. Too many things are going wrong, and it's a bad sign. We've been here long enough."

She had his entire attention now, though he was still too startled to speak. Before he could collect himself, she went on: "Fifteen years is too long, in a place like this. I never meant to get stuck here, I only stayed so long because it was a nice place for you—till you got mixed up with that Howie," she said, implacable. "You and Elva got along fine, she always thought a lot of you, and the place wasn't such a wreck then. And I had a better class of clientele, before the neighborhood got so bad.

"No—we had the best of this place, Roddy. I think the smart thing to do is to think about moving on. I'm sick of it here, and it's no good for you any more, lord knows."

This time she allowed time to go by, time for him to find some reply. He seemed to have trouble speaking.

At last he muttered, "Where do you want to go, then?"

She nodded, perhaps in approval, and said promptly: "I think we might like it out west, in Chicago. A good-sized place wears better, you don't get to feeling so hemmed in, and there's more to do. There's a lot of Elva's folks out there, we could take some of her stuff to them—she's got boxes of trinkets and pictures and I don't know what all, that they'd probably like to have. Besides, they might feel they owe us something, they know well enough how we took care of her these last years. They'd make a good reference, too. I might start out straight housekeeper to some nice old lady. Somebody you'd like, and that would take to you, like Elva did. If she'd had anything to leave, you know you would have got it, Roddy."

She gave a short laugh, startling him.

"But then if she'd had anything to leave, we'd probably had them on our necks all these years. Remember the summer those cousins came by? They didn't waste much time asking questions, did they?"

He seemed bewildered by her reminiscent smile, and turned away from it.

"I don't remember."

"Oh, sure you do. Those two prissy old hens, and the husband of one of them. They were a lot nicer to us when they left than when they came, I can tell you. Took a load off their shoulders, having us here to look out for her, and they knew it."

She stretched—a movement of modified relaxation.

"Who knows, we might even find a place like this, only not so run-down. There's a lot of doctors' widows. A woman will keep her house as long as she can, if she can find someone nice to share with her. You could take up your selling again, too, just for a while. Give you a chance to look over the neighborhoods, and get out and around a bit. I think you need something like that, Roddy. Take away the bad taste of all this crazy stuff with Howie and his bunch—it hasn't been good for you, son. I can tell you that now. You haven't been like I like to see you, not a bit."

"Look . . ." he said, a sudden hard sound without sequel. She waited, but he could find nothing more to do than get up, wander over to the dresser, and stand there turning over the scattered debris of his life here.

Then he said: "You mean we're getting out of here?"

"I think we ought to think about it."

"What happened?" he asked flatly. "She said something? He doesn't think it's Elva?"

"Of course he thinks it's Elva. She probably thinks so herself by now. Just as well." She said, "That's something else I'll be glad to leave behind. She hasn't the personality Elva had, she'd get on our nerves. Can you imagine sitting around having a beer with that one?"

He looked up, finding her in the mirror, where she had already found him.

"What do you mean, leave her behind? You can't leave her behind! You don't think she'll go on saying she's Elva if we're gone, do you?"

"She will if she has any sense," his mother replied calmly. "What else can she do? There's nothing left for her to go back to next door. And that niece isn't going to want to bother about it—come all this way to look at some crazy old lady that claims she's her aunt. Nobody'll listen to her, even if she does try to act up."

But he seemed to take in none of this, and only repeated, in a rising voice: "You can't leave her behind! She was standing right there, that night Sacher came in . . . she saw the whole thing! You think she's going to keep quiet about *that?*"

Her gaze upon him remained calm; but the relaxed, almost indulgent expression with which she had been regarding him hardened.

"Well," she said, "what do you want to do? Take her along?"

He moved away from the dresser, from the mirror, but there was no way of moving out of the ambiance of her steady regard.

Sullen now, not looking at her, he said again: "You can't leave her here if we go."

"You want her to have a little accident? Like the Super?"

His dogged look came up to hers, then fell.

He muttered: "Or like Elva . . ."

"Like Elva!"

After that first, sharp rejoinder, her voice turned unexpectedly mild.

"Now, Roddy—you know better than that. Elva lived out her life, and she had a very peaceful end. Why do you keep going on about her? She wasn't even herself, these last years—sometimes she just about drove you wild, and you know it. Don't be making it different than it was."

He didn't answer.

"Anyway, you're borrowing trouble to worry about Violet. She's a sick old woman, and I don't think myself she's going to pull through. You should have seen her downstairs, today—it wasn't hardly any better than Elva. You get so upset about things I haven't said anything to you, but that's the main reason I think we ought to make our plans. She isn't going to last long."

142

He looked up at her then, finally. But it wasn't a yielding look.

"You won't leave her behind, if we go?"

"No."

She gave in, with that one short sound. He nodded, glum, and sat down again on the edge of the bed. Turning and watching his fingers.

He said, "You weren't really going to, were you?"

"Roddy, I've been watching out for you for over thirty years now, and I haven't let you down yet. But it was a lot easier when you didn't keep nagging at me, and trying to run things yourself. Ever since you met that Howie . . . if you don't know by now you can trust me, you're a mighty foolish boy."

He received this for what it was—all the answer he would get—and said no more. But his mood hadn't lightened. She continued to watch him.

Presently, changing the subject, she said: "What I wish we did know is what happened to Violet's things. That was a nice coat. And it looked like she had some of those old pieces of jewelry, they're starting to bring a good price. Well, it can't be helped. I suppose they've sent them all off to the niece by now. At least we may have got a little nest egg out of it. If we had a will, with the date put back a year or so, I don't see why not. She still writes pretty good."

"Don't do it," he said suddenly.

She had been on the point of getting up, and paused in surprise.

"Don't do what?"

"The passbook. Leave it alone. Get rid of it."

"Don't be so foolish," she said, in deepening surprise. "What's the matter with you? I'm not going to do anything about it while we're here! The whole thing can be handled by some lawyer, from Chicago—there's no hurry."

"*No,*" he said again. "I'm telling you, it's no good. I don't want any tie-up between us and that super."

She did get up then, but with all the relaxation of their talk gone from her manner.

"Roddy, you are the limit," she said. "Any crazy thing Howie wants you to do, you never think twice. And then when it's too late you turn into a nervous wreck and worry *me* to death. There's no use talking to you, these days. Now clean yourself up—you haven't even shaved today! And come down and we'll have some supper," she added, less sharp. "You need some good hot food in you, that's what it is."

He didn't answer, he showed no interest. She hesitated, almost imperceptibly, then left him and went firmly down to the kitchen, knowing that in time he would follow her.

CHAPTER NINETEEN

Back in the forties, when Miss Besserman and her sister (newly widowed) had set up housekeeping together, the two of them had begun to drink a little too much. Especially Miss Besserman. She had always enjoyed a cocktail or two in company; and in the new pleasure of coming home each evening to companionship—and because Juliet needed cheering—she had started bringing home bottles with her. They began with sherry, and went on to experiment with mixed drinks, and it was remarkably cheerful for a while. Dinner later and later; they talked and reminisced—laughed and even wept as they had not done in years, and put a considerable number of chips and cracks in the dinner service. Once Juliet fell down in the kitchen with a casserole. They had laughed themselves speechless over that.

Then a neighbor dropped in on them one evening. It was nearly nine, they had not got around to eating yet, and each found with dismay that it was very difficult to speak to anyone but the other and make sense. The neighbor was very nice about it—assumed there was some celebration, joined them in a drink—possibly went away a little envious. But they themselves had been permanently sobered. It was back to sherry after that—one glass—and dinner at seven sharp.

So now, all these years late, Miss Besserman had discovered her own deterioration in the eyes of a visitor . . . and this time what she had glimpsed had been far more serious. Even frightening.

She had hardly understood a word he was saying. But she knew—from its effect on Mrs. Kay, from some sounding in herself—that she ought to have understood. And taken some warning.

This was what came of eating all that drugged food. Eating it knowingly, indifferently. Perhaps even welcoming the foggy state that it produced, since the frightening night when poor Mr. Sacher had been knocked down trying to help her, and she had been brought back here to a stricter captivity.

That was when she ought to have gathered her forces for a better, more serious try for freedom. She had seen for herself how grave the situation was—how ruthless they could be. Perhaps, if she had not been ill . . . ? But the shock and exhaustion had been too much for her, at first, and then in the languid despair of convalescence she had gone on drifting. Now she knew that she must stop.

Only what had he said?

Her mind was like mush, she thought in a moment of crystal sadness. Her fibers must be soaked with whatever it was they gave her—probably salting it indiscriminately over her food. How long would it take to wear away? And how was she to live meanwhile?

Longing to be able to act, she tried her door and found it open, as it sometimes was in the daytime now. She wandered down to the bathroom and drank cold

water, in hopes of clearing her mind. But it only nauseated her.

They had both gone downstairs, after all that talking,
and the house was very quiet. She stood at the head of
the stairs for a time, unwilling simply to return to her
prison; and gradually the glimmer of an idea came to her.
A memory, really.

Those two keys she had found, on the attic stairs. And
not needed to use. Were they not still where she had
hidden them, in her old room at the front of the house?
She tiptoed back to it, dazedly eager, and made for the
closet on whose shelf she had hidden one of the keys. She
remembered doing that.

Her groping fingers fell into something disagreeable
—but even as she drew them back she remembered what
this was. The macaroni and cheese she had hidden away,
the night of her escape. So she was not completely blank-
minded, after all. And nothing had been disturbed since
then; the key must still be here.

It was. She put it in the pocket of Elva's dress and left
the room, already feeling herself a different person—or
on the road to becoming one.

Just as she reached it, Roddy's door was pulled open.
She had not heard him come back . . . if indeed it was
today that she had heard him go away? The familiar
difficulties began to engulf her again. Oddest of all, for a
moment he seemed as shaken as she was herself.

Then he said: "You looked like Elva. . . ."

She was afraid to answer, afraid not to.

"Do I—?"

He came closer. Her eyes followed him helplessly.

"No—I guess not. It's her dress, though. Isn't it?"

"I don't know. . . ."

He looked at her awhile longer, before making a queer sound—she did not really know what it meant—and going on past her, down the stairs. She heard the front door slam behind him.

The report brought his mother from the back of the house, sharply saying his name. Miss Besserman retreated to her room and shut the door. In a few moments Mrs. Kay could be heard coming upstairs. There was a brief silence, during which Miss Besserman continued to retreat as far as she could—to her chair by the window.

Her door opened.

"Was that Roddy going out?" Mrs. Kay's voice demanded, as if Miss Besserman was somehow responsible.

"What . . . ?"

Mrs. Kay glared at her—without turning to see, Miss Besserman could *feel* that look—before returning abruptly to her son's room. Since she left both doors open, Miss Besserman could hear her rummaging around in there. Not very long, though. She soon came back.

Came in, and sat heavily on the side of the bed.

"Well," she said, her voice flat, "he's gone, all right. In his best suit. You know what that means. Howie."

There was nothing Miss Besserman could say—she did not even know who Howie was—but her silent presence no longer suffered for Mrs. Kay.

"Oh, for goodness' sake, Violet," she suddenly exclaimed. "Stop staring out that window all the time! Turn around and behave like a human being for once!"

But when Miss Besserman's bewildered face came around, the sight of it seemed to exasperate Mrs. Kay still further.

"Sitting there lost in your dreams," she said bitterly. "Very pleased with yourself tonight, aren't you? Roses, and goo-goo eyes, and *balconies!* You've done pretty well for yourself, haven't you?"

What was she talking about?

With a dignity she thought she had lost forever, Miss Besserman asked: "What are you talking about, Mrs. Kay?"

Answered at last, Mrs. Kay let go.

"Don't play sheepie with me, Violet," she said angrily. "There's a lot more going on in that head of yours than you let on, I know that by now. You heard every word he said—what are you pretending for? All of a sudden you're going to be a pampered old lady with that boy bringing you flowers, and holding your hand, and people to wait on you hand and foot—and what's supposed to become of us, when you're up there sitting on your balcony? You don't care about that, do you?"

Clogged and muddied though her mind was, Miss Besserman began to think something worse had happened to Mrs. Kay's. She gathered all her force, and said earnestly: "But *I'm not Elva,* Mrs. Kay!"

Mrs. Kay regarded her with a kind of sour caution.

"Well, if you're not, you're out of luck," she said shortly. "Violet Besserman was buried a week ago, it was in the paper and everything. Where did you think Elva went?

"I'm only telling you for your own good," she went on

presently. Her voice became quiet, as though communication had been established between them at last. "You're old enough to face facts . . . even if Roddy isn't. Things don't always turn out like they should, and you just have to make the best of them, that's all. You'll be all right, if you behave yourself and don't go talking foolish. As far as I can see, you'll be better off then you were before. There's nothing to make a fuss about."

Miss Besserman was not making any fuss.

She said, "Why are you telling me such things? I don't believe you."

"Well, you'd better believe it. That's the way it is. Elva died, and she had to be buried, and she was. You're legally dead, and you'd better get used to the idea."

It was a cruel lie, of course. But breathtakingly cruel. How could any one think of such things to say? She was upset about something Roddy had done; Miss Besserman sensed this. But why should it drive her to tell such mad, cruel lies?

She did not reply, so that Mrs. Kay would not be prodded into more wicked invention. But Mrs. Kay was not going to leave it there.

She went on, in a dogged tone: "She was buried from your place, in your name. What did you think Roddy and I were doing over there, that night you made all the fuss?"

Miss Besserman was shaken into speech. The beginning of speech.

"You . . . took . . ."

"That's right. We took her over there. That's the way it had to be, and that's the way it was. *Somebody* was dead—and it couldn't be Elva, could it?"

"No!" Miss Besserman cried out at last. "It's not true! Mr. Sacher wouldn't *let* them—Mr. Sacher knows that wasn't me! He saw me, he knew me, he wouldn't *let* them—"

"If you mean that superintendent, he left. He didn't want to stay there, after all that trouble you made."

"He isn't gone! You—"

"Oh, he's gone, all right. Use your head, Violet—if he was still there, don't you suppose he'd have said something before now? If he was going to say Elva wasn't you, he'd have said it before she was buried, wouldn't he?"

Would he? Confusion was descending on Miss Besserman again—that awful muzziness she seemed to live with now. She tried to push it back.

"I don't believe she was buried. . . ."

"Now you're being plain silly," Mrs. Kay said. "Of course she was buried. She had to be. Besides, you can read it in the paper—it was in the death notices. I kept it. Violet Besserman."

"No! *No!*"

Mrs. Kay regarded her with glum satisfaction. Her own agitation had gone down as Miss Besserman's increased. Almost friendly, she offered advice.

"There's no use in your going on saying No, no. Why would I tell you this if it wasn't true? You're Elva Ryan now—and lucky to be, if you ask me. You'd better take what goes with it, and keep your mouth shut, or you're just going to end up nobody and nowhere. Instead of in a nice new apartment, with a rich family looking after you! No one's going to believe you're some poor old lady that's been decently buried, they'll just think you're crazy and put you in some kind of a crazy-place. No—you just behave yourself, and you'll be all right."

She got up as she was speaking, her mind already veering to some new idea—her eyes straying toward the door.

"I'll bring you some supper in a minute," she said absently. "You calm down and think it over, you'll see you're pretty well off. Better than we are, the way that family's tricked us. And you don't hear me complaining, do you?"

She went out. Miss Besserman let her go. For a while she sat absolutely still. From long habit—for old comfort —her eyes returned to the glimpse of the apartment house, looming in a sprinkle of lights beyond the garden. Then she gave a choked cry, and pushed herself out of the chair.

Mrs Kay was talking to someone on the telephone as Miss Besserman groped her way hastily downstairs. She turned to watch, but absently, and still speaking.

"Well, you tell him to call home *at once,* if he comes in. It doesn't matter what time. This is his mother."

She hung up, already hunting another number.

"Mrs. Kay—*my things*—"

"Just a minute, Violet."

Dialing, she frowned at Miss Besserman's shaky haste.

"Be careful, will you? There's no hurry. . . . Hello, is this Mike's? Is this Mike?"

Miss Besserman hung on to the newel post through the brief conversation, and the moment it ended she burst out again.

"Mrs. Kay—if this terrible thing is true, you *must tell me*—what—?"

"Oh, be quiet!"

Her mood was worsening again. She gave Miss Besserman a hard stare, and added: "Your trouble is, you've got no one to think of but yourself. You're plain selfish, Violet! Now go back upstairs and don't bother me, I'll be up later."

Dialing again, tight-lipped, she paid no more attention—seemed indifferent to whether Miss Besserman continued to stand there, clinging to her post, or turned away—finally—and went back up the stairs. Her intermittent, impatient voice continued to be audible.

"Is Howie there? It's important—do you know where he is? Well, when do you expect him back? It's Mrs. Kay. Well, when he comes in, you—"

The bedroom door shut, and ended it. Miss Besserman stood in silence, in darkness streaked by the light of the streetlamp. For this was the front bedroom; and she had had in her pocket—and now used—the key that would make it her own sanctuary. Violet Besserman's room. She might starve in it—freeze in it—die there, even; but it would be as herself, as Violet Besserman. If this was all that was left of her, she would defend it as long as she could.

But she would not be Elva Ryan.

CHAPTER TWENTY

N<small>O ONE SLEPT</small> in that house that night except Miss Besserman.

Whether it was the remains of the drug or simple exhaustion, semi-consciousness claimed her as soon as she lay down and clung to her through the growing chill of the night and through Mrs. Kay's several, and severally conducted, assaults on her door.

Her eyes came open, to the words and knocks, but they remained fixed on the ceiling and she made no reply. More efficient than her captors, she had left her key in the lock; and the key Mrs. Kay sent in from the other side met that obstruction. Surprised; annoyed; impatient; placative; at last, quite venomous, Mrs. Kay could only go away again each time. And each time, Miss Besserman drifted back without effort to her dreams.

These were surprisingly vivid and pleasant. Her whole mind, at every level, seemed to have gathered its forces—without any effort on her part—to deny the rumor of her death. Legally she might no longer exist. The small and cherished properties that bolstered that existence might be gone, God knew where. But Miss Besserman lay all that night in a richness of living experience that would have astonished her waking self.

She was all ages, all selves: a running, swinging, child;

an excited girl, stroking out long, long red-gold hair, laughing with someone (who?); Miss Besserman in the warmth and bustle of Flood's Department Store, her domain for so many rewarding years; with Juliet out-of-doors somewhere in fine weather; even with her parents, miraculously restored to loving authority. What flooded back upon her was the *sense* of being alive, always so strong in her, but now distilled into one night's gift, or potion, which she lay and received in half-awareness and still joy.

She did not even mind the constant interruptions of Mrs. Kay's restless night, although she opened her eyes to them many times, and lay quietly regarding the ceiling until they should cease.

It was not only that Mrs. Kay came to her door. She was audible in other ways, dimly recorded by the dreamer. There were occasional loud sounds throughout the house that had no meaning, were forgotten; there was stamping on the porch and door-slamming, and voices that raged in and out of hearing: burst out and died away and burst out again. . . .

All of this shut-out violence Miss Besserman's senses recorded—and ignored. What finally did waken her she had no idea—she was just awake, at some point, lying there in gray light. Chilly; and with silence all around.

Her strange interval of celebration was over. The remnants clung to her—the more so that her mind, at last, seemed clear again. But what a cold, isolated and dead-end prospect it was, to wake up this morning!

Where were all the covers? A turned-back spread showed only mattress; the bed had gone back to disuse.

The closet held only hangers—and a glimpse of white that was, as she well knew, decaying macaroni and cheese. In a bureau drawer, cautiously pulled out, she did discover a knitted afghan—a very nice one that someone had made. Perhaps Elva? She thankfully made a great shawl of it.

Hoping that exhaustion had claimed the Kays at last, she unlocked her door.

It was probably between four and five o'clock—her watch had run down again, alas. In the bathroom, she greeted almost eagerly the scanty-haired wraith in the mirror. She was relieved to see herself looking no worse. And what a blessing it was that they had given up playing games with her dentures!

She went, tidied, downstairs. There was quite enough light at the back of the house to see all she needed to see—even to find, in a cupboard, a jar of instant coffee. Her discovery cheered her beyond reason. She had so longed for coffee, and would not have dared to make it in a pot.

Also, it was warmer here. By the time she had drunk two restoring cups of the coffee and eaten two slices of bread and margarine, her shivering had stopped completely.

Now it was time to think.

She set her watch by the kitchen clock, and determined that never again would she go back into the cloudy world where it was always run down.

Then where should she go?

Mr. Sacher was gone; she believed this. There was no one else in the apartment house whom she cared to appeal to, in these *very* peculiar circumstances. Certainly not at this hour of the morning. Nor was there any such person in the neighborhood. In the shops and stores, yes; but these would not open for many hours.

The buses began to run at six in the morning. There was still change in her purse, so far as she knew. And any of their old neighbors—hers and Juliet's—would gladly take her in and allow her to call her niece (reversing the charges, of course). It seemed to her that this was her best plan. She would simply have to lurk in a doorway until the first bus arrived—hoping that she would meet no rough person, or be picked up by the police.

The police.

Not happily, Miss Besserman considered this idea. She knew where the police station was. She supposed that a police station was always open. They were bound to receive her, surely, even if they thought her a mad old woman escaped from somewhere. Or an old drunk who had been out all night.

But then what?

On the whole, Miss Besserman thought she would rather wait for the bus. If she were *picked up* by policemen, time enough to try and explain herself. But so much better if it could all be done quietly, among friends.

Her bag was still upstairs, in Elva's room. She crept back up and found it—and found, too, the stole she was allowed to wear, as Elva. So she would have an outdoor wrap after all. Ready to leave, she looked in the mirror again for a last adjustment, then shut Elva's door behind her and started down the hall.

A loud thump from Roddy's room froze her to a halt.
Lesser thumps followed, and a crash.

Miss Besserman fled like a cat into the front bedroom
and had barely pushed the door halfway shut behind her
when new thumps sounded, out in the hall. Roddy had
emerged—was flailing his way somewhere.

He crashed into the bathroom, and was very sick.

This went on, with groans and intervals.

Miss Besserman managed to get her door soundlessly
shut, and turned the key. After what seemed a very, very
long time she heard him come out into the hall and
slump somewhere nearby. She could hear him heavily
breathing, still giving an occasional groan. He must be
sitting at the head of the stairs.

He got up again. She heard him go down the hall and
open a door, saying something in a complaining kind of
way. A long pause followed. Muttering, he came back
again and lurched down the stairs, and was presently lost
to hearing.

Miss Besserman drew a long, unhappy breath. A
braver woman, perhaps, would have taken the opportunity to slip downstairs and out of the house. Even if he
heard her go out, he was obviously in no condition to
chase her. But Miss Besserman was not even tempted.

Besides, she half awaited the sound of Mrs. Kay coming out to follow her sick son.

A long time went by, and nothing happened.

Miss Besserman gave up leaning on the wall and went
to sit down, resigned to waiting. At least she knew the
time now. The first bus had already done.

Roddy was coming back. Very slowly, but under better control. She heard him come up the stairs and stand, as if considering what would be a good place to go. To her relief, he decided on the other end of the hall.

Very soon he came all the way back. Tried her door-knob. Miss Besserman shut her eyes.

"Hey," he said, rattling the knob. "Hey!"

She endured it. But when he began a sudden furious thumping and pounding at the door, she could not endure that.

"Oh, what is it? *What is it?* Please stop!" she cried out —and, to her astonishment, he did stop. Gave a sort of grunt, and stopped. Stood there awhile, and then went back down the hall.

Into his room?

Time went by—enough of it so that she dared hope he had flung himself down to sleep again—when, to her dismay, she began to hear him talking.

Arguing—in either his mother's room or his own.

This went on. She could not make out any words, at first—did not wish to; but words and phrases began at last to penetrate to her.

". . . *connections!* They *know* me, around here! You think I'm still some kid you can drag around, like you . . ."

A little later it was about the mysterious Howie. Howie, Howie. ". . . wasn't Howie's fault, it was you! Howie never *said* . . . it was *you* that . . ."

Why was Mrs. Kay putting up with this harangue, without an audible word of disagreement? It didn't seem like her. But then, it didn't seem like the taciturn Roddy. to go on and on as he was doing, either. Clearly some crisis had come upon them.

As for Miss Besserman, there was nothing for her to do but wait. She could not even guess how long, the way things were in the house today. All she could do, once more, was to wait.

And try not to listen.

CHAPTER TWENTY-ONE

BY MONDAY MORNING, Tony had worn out his credit
with all official sources of help.

He wasn't even trying Bingham-and-Bailey again. It
was clear by now that Bailey, however sympathetic personally, wasn't going to move without Mr. Bingham's in-
structions. Mr. Bingham wasn't going to encourage any
direct involvement in the second Mrs. Ryan's problems
if he could prevent it. And Tony's father was on Bingham's side.

After that disastrous Sunday-morning visit, Tony had
gone to him as soon as he got home. The drive back had
given him time to cool, intellectually at least, and he did
not make the mistake of showing any emotional frazzle.
Anger, frustration, alarm would only have served as signals that he was involved in a situation that was better
avoided. His parents were uneasy enough about his new
interest.

So he came home as if from a pleasant excursion, an
interesting visit, and began by giving his father a soften-
ing description of the old house and office. His mother
was the one who showed most response.

"But I don't understand why it's all so Victorian,
dear," she said. "The twenties were terribly modern,
weren't they?"

"I believe he took over someone else's practice," Tony's father said with restraint. "House and all. So it isn't actually your grandfather's house that you've been exploring, you know."

"Well, maybe so," said Tony. "But he did live and practice there for more than twenty years. You'd probably recognize the signs of him better than I."

His father did not reply.

"You'd think she'd have modernized, in all those years," his mother said thoughtfully. She got a direct look from her husband.

"It was probably a question of money. After all, there was child-support for many years, and starting out again with no capital."

Now both mother and son were quiet, perceiving that the subject was still, incredibly, a touchy one. In this solid husband and father still dwelt one of those children who had received support—and perhaps been sent for uncomfortable visits.

Tony risked saying. "Do you remember her at all? Elva, I mean?"

His mother glanced at him rather nervously; but his father surprised them with a short laugh.

"Elva! Yes—of course. Is that Scandinavian? Saxon?"

Tony said boldly, "I'm afraid there isn't enough left of her to guess. She just looks like a nice little old lady—not very happy."

"Poor thing," said his mother, readily sympathetic.

But his father did not say anything.

Tony gave up the idea of proposing Aunt Elva for a visit. To his father's house, anyway. Yet he was still determined to get her away from Brook Street without waiting for the slow and due processes of law, destruction and construction to be achieved. Whatever was wrong there had *not* been going on for years; and he didn't think she was going to survive much more of it.

Yet he was at a hopeless disadvantage in trying to explain his feelings. Reasonable and fair were the watchwords; and they were useless to him now. How did you explain the hard menace of a Mrs. Kay, and that dead-eyed son just barely under control—and Elva herself, deteriorating every time he saw her? Some drastic change had taken place there, and recently—perhaps with the notification from Mr. Bingham. The situation was now intolerable. But he couldn't prove a thing; he could only feel it.

His parents went off on their Sunday visit to his sister and her new baby. He chose to skip these joys and pursue his own problem. After some restless thought, he pursued it into Cambridge, where a friend of his lived off-campus, very snugly, with an elderly Miss Cushing. She had plenty of room in her house, because she took only one young man at a time—for flavor, she said, and some help too. Unconventional herself, she was the only person Tony could think of who might not mind getting involved in the affairs of his step-grandmother.

She didn't much like the idea of having an old lady around, though. Even temporarily. A couple of hours with old ladies, she said, looking him in the eye, and she began to feel like one herself. Why didn't he put her in one of those residential hotels that were full of them?

He explained that Elva wasn't, at the moment, up to

these standards of reposeful gentility.

"She's kind of a refugee," he said frankly. "I don't know what she's been going through, with that creepy pair, but it must have been rough. It wouldn't surprise me if one or both of them had police records."

"Oh, nonsense," said Miss Cushing. "You're just trying to tempt me. Besides—a *step*-grandmother? I never heard of such a thing. What in the world is it?"

After considerable questioning—during which Tony was allowed to put in a lot of bulbs that had come from Breck's—Miss Cushing decided she was curious enough to have Elva after all. Just for a little while—and on the understanding that the boys would be responsible for her. He accepted her terms without hesitation, knowing that the comfortable and well-run house would absorb Elva without any difficulty, and that Miss Cushing was much kinder than she sounded. He was so pleased, so relieved, that Miss Cushing became quite content with them both. She said she was actually beginning to look forward to tomorrow.

"I don't even know if I can get any of her things out," he warned her. "She may just show up in whatever she's got on."

"A ragged shawl, no doubt," said Miss Cushing scornfully. "Now stop embroidering, or I'll begin to think it's all a hoax. What time are you coming?"

He thought it best to ignore his Monday schedule and go directly to Brook Street as early as he could get there and hope to be admitted. Say, ten. That way, if there were any difficulty about his getting in, or getting Elva out, he would have time to work out some new offensive, right on the spot. He found that, like Miss Cushing, he was beginning to look forward to action. That last interview with Mrs. Kay still lay undigested within him.

The morning arrived in cold and foggy rain, Novemberish, which gave his journey a more somber air. He got out of the house with a spare raincoat and umbrella—and a slight feeling of being out of his mind. The town, and Brook Street—and especially his grandfather's house—all struck him as so dismal in this changed weather that he lost most of his sense of adventure on arrival. But not his determination.

The house showed no lights, although lights were burning everywhere else in the dark morning air. Nor did anyone come to answer the front bell. He rang urgently, many times, but raised no flicker of life inside. Finally he knocked hard with the side of his fist.

They had to be there . . . unless they had flown the coop. Taking Aunt Elva? Abandoning her?

A discouraged-looking old Cadillac was parked at the side of the house, at the end of a weedy drive. He went rapidly around this and into the sad back garden. And saw lights on, downstairs.

So they were there.

The kitchen windows were too high to see into, past their half-curtains. He went up on the back stoop and struck the back door as if it were an enemy. It opened at once.

Roddy stared out at him—unshaven, swollen-eyed. In trousers and soiled shirt. He said nothing.

"You know who I am," Tony said. "I want to see Mrs. Ryan."

Roddy shook his head. The door began to close again. "You can't. She's dead."

"Dead!"

At the last moment, he thrust his weight against the door. Indifferently pushed from within, it yielded, and they stared at each other, each holding on.

"She can't be dead! I just saw her yesterday!"

The physical shock of the pushed door seemed to have shaken Roddy to attention.

He said with new force, "I tell you, she's dead. Elva's dead! What do you care?" he added, savage. "It's what you wanted, isn't it?"

And in a sudden powerful heave he shut the door again.

Tony stood there and hammered. Waste motion, completely thoughtless. Rain continued to drip on him. He dropped his arm and ran down the steps, out of the yard. Back to the street again.

He didn't know where he was going, only that shock and disbelief were shooting him into action. But what action? What was he doing?

In front of the house he made himself stop—stand there, rained on, trying to think. The gloomy old house blocked him, deadening thought.

He could go to Bailey now. Absolutely; right now. And have him *call* Mr. Bingham, if he couldn't move without Bingham's say-so. But no more delay. They were going to be back here within the hour—and with police, if necessary.

He took his first real breath and was turning away— sending one more disbelieving glance over the impassive house before him—when he saw her. At the upstairs window again. Standing there.

Standing. And meeting his eyes in one frightened glance, before she turned away. It was so brief a glimpse that it might have been a ghost whom he had surprised, or a projection of his own shocked mind, so full of the thought of her.

But he knew it wasn't.

The hell with Bingham and Bailey. He gave a quick look around the deserted, rain-soaked street, and slipped around to the side of the porch.

CHAPTER TWENTY-TWO

THE LONG-UNPAINTED trellises which endured in the vines' grip would probably crack at the pressure of a hand, let alone a foot. But the vines themselves had thick, branched trunks for climbing. The only question was how securely they gripped the porch roof.

With a fast eye, Tony chose his spot and began to mount. Everything held. No pruning had interfered with this growth for years, so he had to fight his way up through wiry thickets, often clinging to a hold he could not see but only choose by touch and size. Halfway up he became conscious of a general, trembling sway in the whole contraption, and bits of debris began to fall on and around him. At the very top one foothold broke and he dangled awhile, thrusting for another. Luckily, he had on moccasins instead of the sandals; less luckily, he lost one of these somewhere in the vine.

He didn't care. He was up, crouched like a starting racer on the tilted roof. Its condition was appalling. From his crouch he considered what he could grasp to pull himself to, and along, the front of the house. There was nothing but shutters, which he did not trust.

He saw her appear at the nearer window and struggle to raise it.

It went up only a few inches, but that aperture offered

him a good grasp on the inner sill. He made it over to the window and ended up in a secure squat, his face close to hers. She was leaning to his level, and looked very worried. But alive.

"Oh, be careful, dear," she whispered. "I can't get it up any more, there are little pegs—what shall we do?"

"It's all right," he whispered back. "How are you?"

"Oh, much better, thank you! I was going to leave this morning . . ."

"You still are," he promised, and extended one of his hands inside the room. "Show me where the pegs are."

She grasped the hand eagerly in both of hers and guided it upon the inner surface of the frame. His hope was that the pegs would prove to be as decayed as everything else if they got some rough treatment. One was. The other seemed grown into place.

She fluttered away while he was wrenching at it blindly, and came back with a nailfile.

"I think they're both asleep," she whispered, offering him this. "They were up all night. . . . Oh, if I had only known it was you, I could have come down and let you in!"

"*No,*" he grunted. "Just wait—it's coming—"

"Oh, so *dangerous* for you—"

He lost patience and squeezed his shoulders in, thrusting upward. The window yielded so suddenly he lost his balance. There was an awful crash, and he was sprawled half over the sill, head down into the room.

Her frantic hands plucked and seized at him everywhere. In spite of this, and under a flood of little whispers, he got himself ungracefully inside and up on his legs again. It was a good feeling.

But as he opened his mouth to speak to her, she seized his arm in both hands. Began shaking her head violently.

"Wait—wait! They might have heard!"

They might indeed, if they were still in the land of the living. Since he wasn't sure what he meant to do next, he listened too.

Someone was certainly on the move—coming at a rapid pace, almost a run, up the stairs. Not a word spoken or called out—just the fast footsteps by-passing them and diminishing toward the back of the house.

"That's Roddy," she whispered, looking up at him in such fear that his anger began incautiously to waken. He put his arm around her and gave her a little squeeze. The footsteps came back, much slower. They came up to the bedroom door and stopped again.

"What the hell are you doing in there?"

"Nothing—nothing!" she said, so quick and clear that he looked down at her in surprise. Her eyes meeting his, even while she spoke, implored his silence; and he nodded agreement, managing a smile.

Roddy went, slowly, back downstairs.

She was trembling so badly by now that Tony helped her over to the velvet settee and put her down on it. Sat beside her.

"It's all right, don't be afraid," he said, very low. "I'll keep this as quiet as I can. But you do want to leave, don't you?"

"Yes! But I can, I have my key—and you mustn't be, you mustn't let them know—"

She hardly knew what she was saying—and to tell the

truth, he was hardly listening. *Why had Roddy said she was dead?* It hadn't been a taunt; he had simply come out of his stupor and blurted out an angry belief. *And then he came up and spoke to her.*

A chill sense of something more complex than he had supposed nudged at Tony. Mr. Bingham would thoroughly have approved the caution he was feeling now.

"Look," he said, interrupting some breathless endeavor on her part. "It's going to be all right, we are going to leave—today, right away. But will you just wait here a minute while I go down and clear the way? Do you have some things you want to pack?"

There was no way to get her out without meeting them. No way of meeting them without a quarrel, he felt sure. At least she could miss that.

"Don't go down there!"

"It'll be all right—don't worry. You're free to leave, and you're going to leave. Just get yourself ready, and I'll be back for you."

She kept him from rising.

"I'm not Elva."

He looked at her seriously. Her return gaze seemed perfectly sane.

"She died. I'm sorry. My name is Violet Besserman. . . . Miss Besserman," she added, wanly exact.

"But . . . why?"

"They didn't want to lose the house. They—they have a dreadful business here, I can't tell you . . . They use your grandfather's offices . . ."

She forced this out, a necessary warning, and then looked up at him again.

"So you see you mustn't go down. You can't talk to them, they are dangerous people. They hit Mr. Sacher, and knocked him down, when he tried to help me."

The name reverberated around in his mind, not yet meaningful, not yet pursued.

"You mean they've kept you here? Forced you to pretend you were Elva?"

The doubt in his voice was not for her—only that such behavior was possible. But she seemed to take it as a deeply felt reproach. To be unable even to answer.

He went on quickly: "Well, the first thing is to get you out—right? Do you have somewhere to go? Do you live near here?"

She was looking more and more upset.

"I lived next door, but they took Elva over there . . . after she died. They left her in my apartment so people would think it was me. That was the night they knocked Mr. Sacher down. . . . "

Her lips barely moved, trying to explain these horrors to him, and her sad little face never turned from his. There flooded into his mind, from some clue, the newspaper item he had puzzled over in his father's house: the murdered superintendent, the body of the elderly woman who had lived alone. This was what it was all about.

"My God."

He had said it aloud, a kind of groan; and to cover the sound he blundered on: "But they're criminals—these people are criminals!"

She knew that. She only didn't know what to do about it.

Then the thought leaped to mind—was spoken before he realized it: "How did Elva die?"

"I don't know. She wasn't very well, when I came. That was why they . . . wanted me. Perhaps she just died. Or perhaps she had too much of whatever they gave us so we would sleep. I don't think they would have wanted her to die, do you?"

"No," he muttered. "No . . . Never mind, it doesn't matter now. What we have to do first is to get you out of here."

But how?

His swashbuckling ideas, of not more than ten minutes past, now seemed insane. This was not the house to appear in, an accusing surprise, and announce that Mrs. Ryan was now coming away with him and what did they propose to do about it? They had already answered that question, in the apartment house. And while it was probably true that Mrs. Kay was a woman, she wasn't the kind who wrung her hands while the men fought. He could count on two of them. And nothing barred.

Across the room the rain blew in through the window of his entry. Neither one of them had thought to close it. Could he possibly get her out there, lower her gently from that roof? A tiny vision of them engaged in this activity was enough to end that idea.

He gave a small sigh—managed a smaller smile to follow it.

"Well, let's think," he said. "There's a way. We'll find it."

CHAPTER TWENTY-THREE

WHAT HE HAD to do first was to reconnoiter.

The worst part of starting this was to get away from Miss Besserman, who clung to him with all her might. She implored him to go back out the window. She promised to use her key, to slip out at the first opportunity—there were many, she moved about the house almost as she liked now! If they came across her downstairs they thought nothing of it any more. But if they saw him—!

He had only to wait in his car, outside. She *promised* to get out, now that someone would be waiting for her.

His own temptation was to climb back out and go for the police. But if he were heard or seen getting out again, what price Miss Besserman? She didn't know how little they had to lose, how finally they had "knocked down" her Mr. Sacher. He was afraid there would be no old-lady witness waiting there for him when he got back.

One thing he was grateful for: she was not a hysterical type. Flutter and clutch she might; but there was a sound and sane mind in that little skull, as he had known there would be, and he could talk to her honestly and calmly. At last she let go, and allowed him to turn the key. But she didn't turn it again behind him, though he had tried to make her promise to do so. In fact, she reopened the door a tiny crack.

174

He had got rid of his remaining moccasin; but the hall floor still creaked a bit. He was counting on the Kay's being divided, engaged in separate activities—because while there had been sounds of someone moving around below Miss Besserman's room, in the hall or the doctor's offices, there had been no talk. He thought those two wouldn't work together, the length of time he had heard them, without so much as a word spoken.

The sliding doors were separated. He could see part of the office, and could gauge more certainly where the sounds were coming from—which was the back part, the surgery. He decided to leave this situation as it was, for the moment, and find the other one.

The stairs divided at the landing, and he silently took the back steps—came with Indian caution upon an empty kitchen, and through that to the other unoccupied downstairs rooms. Puzzled, he backtracked. They were getting ready to leave: a miscellaneous heap of possessions stood by the back door, suitcases, boxes, a couple of coats, all waiting to be taken out to the car, he surmised.

Plus any useful instruments and drugs from the doctor's surgery.

He felt he understood the situation now, except for the excessive quietness of their preparations. Why did it make all that difference whether Miss Besserman heard them or not?

Uneasy, he went back upstairs. The front bedroom door suddenly revealed his old lady, wordlessly imploring him to come back. He gave her a mysterious wave, and went on toward the back of the house. Bathroom open and empty; man's room churned to chaos, no one there. Attic stairs. Two closed doors at the end.

He considered these awhile before trying them. Measured his chances of surprising and subduing the amazon Mrs. Kay before her son could get up here. He thought it a chance that had to be taken, unless he was willing to sneak back and sit with Miss Besserman until they left. Or until both Kays came for her.

Not much choice. He eased a knob around, and peered into a small, empty room. Empty of people. A white-painted bed and an empty wheelchair said this was where his grandfather's widow had spent her last days. He looked, and moved on.

Next door Mrs. Kay was lying on her bed. Fully dressed. He saw her shoes first, and a solid black-clad arm that hung over the edge. A broken glass lay on the floor near the window, where tireless rain made the only sound in the room.

He came in slowly—came over and looked down at her, seeing that her open eyes fixed on the wall had already lost the look of human tissue. Were like artifacts, like plastic replacement. Her black dress was twisted and torn around the neck; the neck itself had something wrong with it.

He backed out.

In silence, the door re-closed, he got himself turned around and headed back down the hall. The old lady, in ever widening glimpses, reached out for him as soon as he was near enough and he let her draw him into the room beside her. He turned the key himself, and then stood as though considering it.

176

"Oh, I'm so glad you're back, Tony!"

She had scrupulously stopped touching him, as soon as he was safe with her, but she hovered very close. Her anxious face remained at the corner of his eye, he could neither meet it nor avoid it. Or speak.

"Oh, what is it, dear? *They saw you?*"

"No, no."

He wandered away, escaping her for the moment, and found himself sitting on the velvet settee again. She came and crouched beside him, not speaking until he managed to look at her.

"Something bad?" she whispered.

He took her hand, which was very cold. She was, in fact, shivering. The damned window still blew all outdoors on them—evidently she hadn't dared touch it, for fear of more racket. He wasn't going to tackle it either. He reached out for the bedspread, pulling it free and wrapping it around her.

Saying carefully, as he did so, "They're leaving. Getting out. It won't be long."

"Oh. Oh! *Then they're taking the doctor's things*—that's what they're doing!"

He could only nod. After a minute he put his arm around her, probably as much for his comfort as hers, and waited as her shivering began to subside. Sat on, waiting. In obedient quiet, she waited with him.

The fact that he knew very little about fear wasn't much to his credit. Nothing particularly fearful had happened to him. What challenges had come up so far in his life had been half pleasurable. Fear was a thrill, a chance, a narrow squeak; you could handle it if you kept going and kept your head. He had never before conceived of fear as a total, nauseated revulsion. So it took him a while to realize what was the matter with him.

Realizing helped. A little.

By the time they heard Roddy coming upstairs again he was able to get Miss Besserman up and unwound from the bedspread and over to the closet. He wanted her out of the way of whatever happened, but she wasn't following the idea—he had to push her in, gently, and her confusion made it awkward. By then Roddy was rattling the door.

"Hey, Violet—open up. Here's your breakfast."

She didn't believe this for a moment—no one would have—but that was too bad. Her fear turned almost to panic.

"Oh, what does he want—?"

A shoulder assault on the door was her answer.

The closet door shut on her whisper, her terrified face. He made it across the room in several soundless strides—took breath, turned the key, and yanked the door wide open. Surprise had to give him the lead.

He took it in a shameless belly-slam, to the man who stood gaping there, and followed this with the best uppercut he could organize.

Roddy fell on the floor and lay there.

It wasn't believable. He stood there a second, lost—leaned over to peer, straightened up again fast, and felt his knees shaking. Miss Besserman had somehow come into view and was staring. He stared back at her.

Then he put out his hand. She came toward him like a mechanical grandmother doll, and he reached out and lifted her over Roddy. Without one word, or one look behind them, they went downstairs together and out of the house.